KATIE WATSON AND THE PAINTER'S PLOT

MEZ BLUME

RIVER OTTER BOOKS

First published 2017 by River Otter Books

PB ISBN: 978-1-9999242-0-1
EBook ISBN: 978-1-9999242-1-8

For Mom and Dad, who raised me on daily, healthy doses of the things that matter most, like good stories.

NOTE FROM THE AUTHOR

For those readers among you who know a bit about history, you might recognise a few real-life characters in this story, for example King James I, Queen Anne of Denmark and William Shakespeare.

These and other characters in the book belong to History, and, while I tried to give them an accurate and fair representation, their words and deeds in the following pages are all purely made up.

Nevertheless, you might just discover quite a few things about life in Shakespeare's England through Katie's adventure. After all, there is no better portal to the past than a book!

THE DOOMED SUMMER

"*H*ave a good trip," I told Fergie and Francis as I pushed a bowl of pellets into their crate. "At least *you'll* be going on an adventure this summer. Not like some of us." Fergie squeaked, which might have been sympathy in guinea pig language. But judging by their blank expressions as they furiously nibbled their pellets, I wasn't convinced they really understood how I was feeling.

There was a *ding dong* from the doorbell. "That'll be your ride," I informed the guinea pigs. I hoisted my duffel bag over one shoulder, then squatted to pick up the crate from its place below the hooks where all my riding ribbons hung. As I stood up, the ribbons brushed against my hair, as if to tease me. I gritted my teeth and turned away.

Waddling down the hallway, I stopped in front of Charlie's room. His door was open, but he had his back to me, taking the posters from his wall and rolling them up for packing. The room looked as sad and bare as an undecorated Christmas tree. The sight of its blandness made me feel hollow and lonely, like things would never be the same again. Why did this summer ever have to come?

Normally, summers couldn't come soon enough. I would count down the days on my horse wall calendar until we could pack up our bags and head off to England to visit my grandparents. Charlie and I call them Nan and Pop, and we've spent every summer with them since I was born. That was part of "the deal" when my English mum agreed to marry my dad and move to America.

Summers in England really are superb. Nan and Pop live in an old farm house in Kent with woods, blackberry brambles, an old barn and even a wishing well. Charlie and I always played orphans out there, pretending to live in the barn and throw wishes into the well that one day we would live in a palace with servants to bring us tea and extra buttery scones on silver trays whenever we liked. Then, when Nan called us into the house for tea time and brought us a tray of fresh baked scones, we'd imagine *she* was our servant and laugh at our secret joke. Nan said we were cheeky, but always with a smile.

Of course our games became more sophisticated later on, when I got old enough to start reading murder mysteries. Then Charlie became Sherlock Holmes and I was his right-hand man, Watson; we'd think up all kinds of crimes to solve around the farm and the village.

As I stood there remembering it all, the crate tipped, and one of the guinea pigs gave a loud, complaining *reek*. I moved away from Charlie's open door before he could turn around. I didn't feel like talking; and anyway, all he ever talked about these days was the new life awaiting him in Scotland and all the exciting things he planned to do at university. He didn't have time for silly games with an eleven-year-old sister anymore. He had *real* adventures to look forward to now.

I hobbled downstairs. Dad had got to the door first and was chatting to Miss Thaxton. When she noticed me, her eyes widened and her mouth stretched into an unusually toothy smile.

"Hi there, Katie. Now don't you worry about those guinea pigs. They are going to get *loads* of attention up at the barn while you're away. The kids will adore them."

"I know," I said, then added a "Thank you." We stared awkwardly at each other for a second before I finally got the nerve to ask the question burning in my throat. "How's Gypsy?"

With that over-the-top smile plastered on her face, Miss Thaxton answered, "Oh, he's great!"

"Is anyone, you know … riding him these days?" I asked with dread nibbling at my stomach.

Miss Thaxton still smiled but looked pityingly at the same time. "He has a new rider, yes. But Katie, Gypsy will never forget you. I've seen hundreds of riders and horses; you two have a truly special bond. And when you get back from your summer travels, you know you can always come and visit him, don't you?"

I swallowed and nodded, then slipped quietly into the dining room while Dad carried the guinea pigs out to Miss Thaxton's truck.

I let my duffel bag drop to the floor and sank into my

chair at the table. Mum set a bowl of porridge down in front of me. I could feel her eyeing me, the way she does when she knows I'm upset but doesn't want to set me off on one of my "contrary moods."

"Raisins?" she asked brightly.

I shook my head.

"Maple syrup?"

I poked at the lumps of oats and shook my head again.

"Don't be silly. You love raisins and maple syrup."

Without looking at Mum, I reached down and pulled the mystery novel I was reading from my duffel bag. Propping it open on the table, I pretended not to notice as she sprinkled raisins and syrup into my porridge.

"How's the book?" she asked.

I shrugged and grumbled, "Better than *real* life."

"Oh? Real life's not so bad, is it? After all, we're flying to England tomorrow, and then who knows what sort of fun Nan and Pop have planned for you all?"

"You and Dad and Charlie will be having all the fun up in Scotland." I should've stopped there, but there was still a lot of steam inside me that needed venting. "I *still* don't see why I have to stay behind while you 'settle him in' and go hiking and see otters and puffins and … and …"

"You know why, Katie," Mum chided in a gentle voice. "This is a special time for Charlie. And besides that, the doctor thinks you need to take it a bit easy until we're sure you're 100 per cent recovered. You'll have a chance to visit the Highlands some time. In the meantime, why not at least *try* to enjoy your holiday with Nan and Pop? They're *so* looking forward to spending time with you."

"It's still not fair," I grumbled under my breath and leaned over my book with my head in my hands.

With one stealthy movement, Mum slipped the book out from under me and turned it over to look at the back cover. "A mystery, eh? This does look good. Have you ever noticed that in books ... the good ones, at least ... the main character has to go through difficulties, sometimes enormous, challenging changes out of their control?"

I didn't answer, but Mum carried on. "Isn't *that* what sets the adventure going? All the change and challenge? Isn't *that* what makes it a story worth reading?" She handed me back the book. "Just something to think about."

Then she turned right on her heels and started scrubbing the porridge pot before I had the chance to exercise my contrary mood. *So frustrating that we are so much alike*, I thought. From our lanky limbs and strawberry-coloured hair to our love of riding horses. Mum always knows what I'll argue back before I do and always has me blocked.

I knew what I wanted to say. *Maybe* that's how it worked in books — *maybe* characters have to go through all sorts of rubbish to get their adventures. But it didn't make me feel any better, and it certainly didn't persuade me that having my life turned upside down was any kind of adventure worth having.

I forced down my porridge and carried the bowl to the sink. Mum wiped her hands on the tea towel and walked over to my duffel bag at the same time. "Are you sure you've packed everything, Kate? I don't want Nan having to go to the shops a dozen times for things you've forgotten." She leant down to pick up the bag and let it drop into the chair with a grunt. "My heavens! What have you got in here? Your entire library?"

"It's just clothes and a few books," I spat out, rushing over. But before I could step in, she'd unzipped the bag and found them: the riding helmet and boots I'd stuffed right down at the bottom, hoping they'd stay hidden there until Mum and Dad and Charlie went off to Scotland and left me alone with Nan and Pop. Mum would never agree to let me go to riding camp; she would want me to follow the doctor's orders and take it easy. But if I asked my grandparents nicely enough, they were sure to give in. At least they would have done. Now I was busted.

"Katie, what is this?" She held out the riding helmet, her eyebrows raised and waiting for an explanation.

"I just thought I could try again over the summer. I won't have anything else to do."

"Katie …"

"Mum, I *know* I can do it if I just—"

"KATIE!" Mum took a deep breath, then spoke in a low, calm voice. "We've been through this. I know how badly you want to ride again. And I admire your determination, I really do. But, love, maybe you're just not ready *yet.*"

I looked away from her, a puff of hot air fuming from my nostrils.

She took a step nearer and stroked my hair, the very patch of hair that hid the large, uneven scar across my scalp. "Your accident with Gypsy was a terrible, traumatic thing to go through. Most girls would never dream of riding ever again after that. Be patient with yourself. The time will come. There's no need to rush it."

I jerked back from her hand. "But I *am* ready! I've *got* to ride, Mum. You don't know what it's like not being able to do the thing you love most in the world!"

Mum looked uncertainly at me for half a moment. Maybe she was coming around after all!

Then she shook her head, and my heart sank. "I'm sorry, Katie. I don't want you going near a horse while your dad and I are away. Nan and Pop wouldn't know what to do if something happened, and ... I just ... I don't want you getting hurt again."

My eyes started stinging, and I could feel my chin quivering. Everything seemed to be caving in on me all at once, and I lost it. "It's not fair!" I shouted as my eyes went blurry. "Gypsy was my best friend, and I've lost him. Now Charlie's going away forever, and you're leaving me alone all summer and won't even let me *try* to ride again!"

Charlie chose just that moment to saunter into the kitchen with his hiking pack strapped to his back and ask, "How do I look? Ready to take on the Highlands?"

Mum gave him a look that meant *not now, for Pete's sake*. I wish she hadn't. It only made him take note of my red face and puffy eyes. I spun away from Mum, still standing there holding my riding helmet, pushed past a speechless Charlie and his hiking pack, and ran out of the front door, narrowly missing Dad as he walked up the driveway. I didn't stop until I got to the old tree swing in the backyard.

I couldn't stand it. I knew when the others felt sorry for me — the poor little girl who fell off her horse and went into shock every time she tried to get back on. I *used* to be good! Gypsy and I used to ride like champions, to jump, to fly! Now I was just a pathetic eleven-year-old with a scar on her head and a sheltered, adventure-less life.

Everything had changed for me. Everything felt so uncertain … except for one thing. Unless a miracle happened, this summer would be the worst of my life.

2

OTTERLY MANOR

*T*he journey to England felt like old times. Charlie and I imagined everyone we met on the plane was a suspect in our made-up murder mystery. Once I laughed so hard, my complimentary Sprite came gushing out my nostrils, and then we both laughed so hard the flight attendant came to check everything was alright. I almost managed to forget the wretched reality: this was the last time we'd be going to Nan and Pop's together before everything changed.

But all the old tummy knots came back as soon as Pop collected us at the airport. Of course I was happy to see him; but on the drive home, I wished he would just talk about the weather or anything other than the upcoming trip to Scotland and how magnificent the Highlands would be this time of year. If I'd felt the bitter sting of missing out before, by the time we got to the farmhouse, I was boiling with it.

Nan set out tea for us in the conservatory, but I could hardly enjoy my buttery scone loaded with clotted cream and jam. All she wanted to talk about was Charlie's big move to university and all the wonderful experiences he would have. I found I'd lost my appetite and held the second half of my scone under the table until Oscar, my grandparents' cocker spaniel, stealthily put it away with one, wet chomp.

After tea, Pop had the brilliant idea of pulling out some of his old trekking photos from the attic to show Dad and Charlie. Normally, I never miss a trip up to the attic. You never know what mysterious object from the past you may find up there, from my great grandmother's gramophone with its huge copper trumpet to Mum's collection of riding trophies. But this time I hung back to help Nan and Mum clear away the tea things.

"Are you feeling alright, Katherine?" Nan eyed me sideways and pursed her lips the way she always does when she's being shrewd, making her dimples twice as deep. "I must say, you look a tad flushed."

I shrugged as I handed her a stack of plates. "Just tired from the journey, I guess."

"I don't doubt you are! Why don't you go upstairs and have a lie down until dinner? It won't do to have you coming down with a fever. Pop and I have planned some lovely Days Out for the three of us."

A *Day Out* is Nan and Pop's code word for an educational trip: visits to museums, historic monuments, famous gardens, the occasional castle. All interesting in their own way, and Charlie and I always find a way of turning Days Out into live action detective stories. But a Day Out to some old building with no Charlie to joke around with?

That was hardly the sort of adventure I was looking for, the sort my life seriously lacked.

Nan carried on, happily scrubbing away at the plates. "Pop discovered a really fine old house that's been sitting right under our noses all this time in a neighbouring village. Otterly Manor, it's called. Have a look beside the telephone, Katherine. I do believe Pop's got a brochure about it." She craned her head around and nodded towards the little table under the telephone. "Would you believe, it was built in the sixteenth century and such a specimen! We thought we'd go and explore it tomorrow after we drop this lot off at the station. What do you think, Katie dear?"

I forced what I hoped appeared to be a believably genuine smile.

"You see, Katherine?" Mum piped in. "An adventure already budding!"

I turned my head so Nan wouldn't see me roll my eyes.

Mum shot me a stern glare back, but transformed it magically into a smile as Nan turned around from the sink.

I felt a little ashamed, but I was also fed up. "C'mon, Oscar. Let's go outside," I said, patting my leg so he would follow me. Reluctantly, I picked up the brochure on my way to the door with no intention of actually looking at it, but to keep Nan happy. But after a few minutes of sitting on the wishing well, looking blankly down into its black depths, I unfolded the brochure and let my eyes skim over it. They travelled immediately to the words *Riding at Otterly Manor*, and my heart gave a little leap. I continued reading hungrily. *Otterly Manor boasts one of the largest remaining royal hunting grounds in the country. Experience riding horseback like the ladies and lords of old at Otterly Manor's Equestrian Centre.*

I folded the brochure back up and wedged it into my pocket. I wouldn't dare let Mum see this. She had said I was strictly to stay away from horses; but surely it couldn't hurt me just to go and *look* at them, could it?

Yes, it could. I knew it would be torture to come so close yet not be able to ride. But that didn't matter. I needed to be near horses ... to prove to myself that I wasn't afraid so I could prove it to Mum and everyone else. For just a moment, I allowed my imagination to paint a picture of me on Gypsy, galloping across an ancient forest. It was just a thought, but the thought alone was so exhilarating, I now felt tomorrow's Day Out to Otterly Manor couldn't come soon enough.

THE NEXT MORNING, the dreaded goodbyes came and went in the dreary, dewy dawn at the train station. Being left behind still stung, but now part of me was eager to see them go.

"Be good, Katie," Dad said. "We'll be thinking of you all the time."

"Keep a sharp eye on things, Watson," Charlie said. "And here. This is for you." He handed me a tatty, pocket-sized, leather-bound book with *The Hound of the Baskervilles* embossed in gold on the binding.

"But this is *your* copy. I can't take it."

"Yours now. I'm promoting you to head detective in my absence. Just don't forget to write me with all the juicy mysteries you unravel." He smiled and ruffled up my hair. I clutched the book to my chest with a lump in my throat.

Lastly, Mum pulled me into a tight hug, then held both my forearms so we were eye-to-eye. "*Try* to enjoy yourself, Katie. You never know what may happen." She smiled, then added with extra emphasis, "And Katie, please, *be careful.*"

I hugged Mum and waved them off as the train pulled away. But all I could think was how much I *didn't* want to *be careful.* I didn't want to be babied. I wanted an adventure, and I was going to have to find one. Maybe one would be waiting for me at Otterly Manor …

3

I SPY

*B*ack at the farmhouse, Nan and Pop appeared to have forgotten all about our plans for a Day Out. They both settled down in their chairs to read the papers. I inwardly groaned as I stalked up to my bedroom and took Charlie's leather copy of *The Hound of the Baskervilles* from the bedside table. Curling up under my duvet with Oscar sprawled across my feet, I tried to get lost in the story of a wealthy heir who begs the help of Sherlock Holmes and Dr. Watson when he is cursed by a demon dog. But a few pages in, I gave up and put the book down. It wasn't that the story was boring — I'd loved every Sherlock Holmes mystery I'd read so far, and this was Charlie's favourite. But reading it then only gnawed at the miserable, discontented feeling in the pit my stomach. I didn't just want to *read* an adventure ... I wanted to *live* one. That imaginary picture of me and Gypsy galloping across the royal hunting ground reappeared in my mind like a cruel joke. *Like that was ever going to happen.* I squeezed my eyes shut, thinking maybe I would just sleep the summer away, curled up in my nest like Fergie and Francis, but all alone … a lonesome little hibernating rodent.

My hibernation plan came to a swift end.

"Katherine?" Pop rapped his knuckles once on the door before poking his head around to look in on me. "Feel up to an outing? Nan's packed a picnic to write home about. My own rhubarb crumble for dessert," he added, his bushy white eyebrows wiggling up and down. They stopped wiggling and knitted together. "Unless of course you're feeling poorly?"

"No," I said, pushing the duvet back and swinging my legs to the floor. "I'm fine. I'll be right down." Eager to set off, I stuffed my spy journal down into my backpack, then picked up *The Hound of the Baskervilles* and fanned my thumb through its gold leaf pages. "Why not?" I thought, and nestled it down into the bag as well. It could be a good distraction if things didn't go so well with the horses.

ALTHOUGH WE SPENT every summer in England, it always took me by surprise just how grey and bleak the days could be. Still, the countryside glowed emerald green against the grey sky, and the hedgerows and little village gardens were in full summer bloom.

At the end of a quaint village road lined with gift shops, tea shops and pubs, Pop turned into a drive with a gatehouse. Tall, cast-iron gates barred the way. A lady with a name badge strolled drowsily out of the gatehouse and scanned a card Pop held out to her.

"Welcome to Otterly Manor," she said, half yawning.

Next thing, the gates creaked open and we were driving down a green, sweeping valley carpeted in patches of thick bracken.

"Keep your eyes open." Pop nodded towards the window. "Otterly Manor boasts one of the country's oldest deer parks. Been here since medieval times. If you're lucky, you'll spot the white hart himself."

"If you spot the white hart, you *will* be lucky, as the old superstition has it," Nan added.

I peered out of the window, looking for movement in the bracken. Sure enough, as the road wound upward through a lane of massive, gnarled oaks, I spotted a rack of antlers protruding up through the high undergrowth. The stag trotted forth, completely unafraid of our car, and Pop stopped the car as he led his family of downy does and speckled fawns in procession across the road to graze on the other hillside.

"Wow!" I caught myself mouthing before I remembered that Dad and Mum and Charlie would soon be seeing wild reindeer that would probably dwarf these little tame ones. But these park deer *were* pretty, and I told Pop so when I caught his eyes smiling at me expectantly through his bushy white eyebrows in the rear-view mirror.

The road threaded upwards through the trees until it levelled out onto a wide, flat meadow that had partly been turned into a gravel car park. As soon as Pop turned onto the gravel in search of a parking space, we saw it, straight ahead: a monstrosity of stone soared up out of nowhere. The house — if you could even call it a house — was much grander than I'd imagined. With its great, stone face, stacks of chimneys, crenellated towers and turrets all piled up on top of each other, it was more of a cross between a castle and a town.

"Here we are!" Nan chirped as Pop turned off the engine. "What do you think of it, Katherine?"

"It's … big," was the most creative response I could come up with at that moment.

Pop chuckled. "Big is right! We're going to need our vittles before we tackle the inside. Winny, how about those sandwiches?"

Finishing my sandwich and swigging down the last gulp of ginger beer, I shivered and pulled my hands inside my hoodie, hugging my body with my handless arms. Cold as I was, I was dying to go off in search of the riding centre. *We must be close*, I thought; and as the thought crossed my mind, I heard the wonderful sound of a horse whinny in the distance. I strained my eyes to see through the oak trees and could just make out the bobbing movement of cantering horse and rider in the distant meadow.

"I know what'll warm you up," Pop said, snapping me out of my trance. "Let's give Oscar some exercise, then we'll head for the house. What do you say, Katherine?"

I nodded. "Looks like there's a big field over there," I said, pointing to the meadow where I'd seen the horse.

Nan stayed behind to tidy up the picnic while Pop and I took Oscar to play. Pop found a field much closer to the house than the meadow where I'd seen the rider, but at least it gave me a good view of the Manor's old stables, now used as a warehouse for storing old displays and gardening tools.

Oscar went wild when Pop produced his tennis ball in its plastic sling. Pop knows I love dogs, so he always lets me take charge of slinging the ball. I held the sling back behind my head, then flung it forward, catapult style, sending the tennis ball soaring like a home-run hit. Oscar shot forward to catch it just before it hit the ground.

After a few minutes of the chase, Oscar was panting and my socks were properly soaked through. I stuffed the ball sling into my backpack and hoped Pop would suggest stopping by the café; but he said it was time to find Nan and warm up inside the house.

The only trouble was, inside the vast, cavernous stone house felt even colder than outside! We walked through the first gate tower into a grassy courtyard with marble statues. On the opposite side of the courtyard, we were met by another mass of stone towers, turrets and latticed windows. Then through another passage into a stone courtyard where a sign with an arrow pointed to an arched doorway in a wall decorated with antlers like an old hunting lodge. *Finally*, following the arrow, we entered the house … or a tiny part of the house, anyway.

Just inside, an ancient-looking man in a thick winter coat greeted us in the dark passageway, dabbing his elongated nostrils with a handkerchief. "Welcome to the Great Hall of Otterly Manor. The tour begins here and is self-guided. Oh, and for the little girl …" He picked up a booklet from a side table and offered it to me with a soppy smile. It had a silly cartoon drawing of a young girl in frilly clothing on the cover. A speech bubble came from her mouth with the invitation, *"Can you spot these missing objects in the house? Put an X beside each object you find to win a rubber at the end of the tour."*

"Good luck, ducky," the old man said. "Extra points for

finding the Green Man. He's a tricky one to spot." And he gave me a wink that looked rather like he'd got something in his eye.

"Thanks." I smiled, then promptly turned away, dropping the smile and stuffing the pamphlet into my hoodie pocket. Honestly, why did everyone seem to think I was a baby? I didn't want to spot missing objects. In fact, I didn't want to be in that draughty old house at all. All I could think about was the horse and rider I'd seen out on the grounds, unaware of the wind and drizzle as they galloped across green meadows. Meanwhile, here I was playing a game of *I Spy* all to win a stupid pencil eraser.

Nan and Pop had already started their self-guided tour in the next room, which, according to the plaque on the wall, was the Great Hall, and I could hear them whispering in raptures over every little detail through the doorway. I scuffled along after them, my wet tennis shoes squeaking against the chequered stone floor tiles. Once inside, my eyes travelled automatically up and up to the high, wooden ceiling that reminded me of a honeycomb, then around the walls where dozens of life-sized portraits hung.

Ok, I had to admit, it *was* a pretty impressive dining room. Of course, it would have been better had there been a fire in the gigantic hearth. And better still had Charlie been there to laugh at the ridiculous-looking people in the portraits, especially the man in the stiff, silk suit with a lace collar, high-heeled shoes with big bobbles on top and a silly, pointed goatee beard. An engraved golden plate on the frame informed me the frilly man was the Second Earl of Dorset. If only Charlie had been there, he'd have made up the most wonderful whodunit scenario. *Was it Mr Fancy Pants with the fire poker in the Buttery? Or was it Lady Pugnose with a hairpin in the Orangery?* Just the thought of what Charlie would say made me giggle the tiniest of private giggles, yet it echoed around the cavernous room, right up to the honeycomb ceiling. One of the wardens — a poodle-haired old lady — gave me a disapproving scowl, and I was all too glad to follow Nan and Pop out of the Great Hall and into the Great Staircase.

I must say, I felt a small blip of excitement walking up that staircase. It was one of those wide, wooden ones with heavy banisters like the deck of a pirate ship. The walls were painted with interesting designs of dogs and birds, lounging ladies and musical instruments. And at every turn, a wooden leopard perched on top of the banister posts, showing off a coat of arms.

"What's with all the leopards?" I whispered to Pop who was inspecting a pane of stained glass.

"Oh, that." Pop grinned, always pleased for the chance to show off a bit of trivia knowledge. "That, you see, is the heraldic symbol of the Buckville family. Thomas Buckville, the First Earl of … er, what was it?" He took his glasses from his coat pocket and quickly consulted his guidebook. "Ah, that's it. First Earl of Dorset. Anyway, he had the leopards installed when he took over the place and redecorated it."

"Oh," I said, trying to sound impressed.

The Great Staircase led to a long passage, and I do mean *long*, as in bowling alley long! Not only was it long, it was dark and creepy, and, as Mum would say, "wonderfully wonky". The floors sloped one way, the walls another. And creepier still, all down the wood-panelled walls hung old portraits of stuffy, sombre-looking gentlemen and ladies in what looked to me to be very uncomfortable clothing. I walked hastily along the wonky gallery towards the only source of light at the very end, but I couldn't shake the feeling that all those eyes followed me, marking my every squeaky step.

I was glad to leave the portrait gallery, but my goodness! This house went on forever like a maze! There was bedroom after parlour after airing room; you name it and there was a room for it in Otterly Manor. And Nan and Pop couldn't seem to get enough of rooms!

At last we came to another large, much more open gallery with billiard tables and lots more huge, hanging paintings. A medium-sized one in the corner caught my eye. It was of a girl, about my own age probably, but dressed just like a little queen with golden braids woven tightly around her head. Still, she didn't have the same snooty look as most of the other portrait characters. Somehow she was so lifelike, like someone I might make friends with at school. Her round, rosy cheeks gave her a kindly look and her face sparkled with a pair of clever blue eyes, though there was a speck of sadness in them as well. A bird perched on her finger, and her other hand rested on the head of an enormous grey dog.

My imagination had just begun to play with the thought of what it would be like to live in that golden-haired girl's world when I heard Nan whispering excitedly to Pop behind me. Nan collects special porcelain pieces, and she had just come across a glass case full of what must have been *extra* special pieces by the look on her face. A hefty warden sitting nearby stood up and approached the case with a smug look of information. Sure enough, the three of them were deep into plates, wash basins and figurines before you could say "China". There was no doubt about it — I was going to be stuck in this musty gallery *for eternity*.

I tried to pass the time by peering out of the latticed window at the end of the hall in hopes of seeing the horse and rider again. I had no luck, though, so instead I tried matching up the different outbuildings to their labels on a plaque in the window ledge. By the time I'd spotted the stables, the kitchen garden, the dairy, the jail and the brew-house, all three times each, my stomach had started grumbling. *When would this tour finally come to an end and a trip to the café?*

I felt so antsy waiting that, without really thinking, I pulled the *I Spy* pamphlet from my hoodie pocket and thumbed through it. There was the leopard statue; I put an X in the box beside it. To my surprise, the next page featured the painting of the girl with the big grey dog that had caught my eye. The caption beside it just said *Portrait of Sophia Brunswick-Lüneburg, 1606*. I put an X beside Sophia's portrait, and kept flipping.

A few pages later, I stopped to look at a rather funny-looking object. At first it looked just like a wreath of leaves carved into wood, but on a second take, a pair of eyes, a flat nose and grinning lips appeared right in the middle of the foliage with leaves growing out of its nostrils and mouth and forming his leafy eyebrows. *Green Man* was all the caption said. So *that* was what the old man at the door was on about. I peered up from the booklet at Nan and

Pop; they still had all ears on the warden who was now treating them to a full lecture on each and every painting in the gallery. All the other visitors had moseyed on to other parts of the never-ending house. I shrugged, telling myself I was only playing this baby's game because there was nothing better to do. But truth is, I felt just a little bit excited about finding this mysterious Green Man who was supposedly so tricky to spot. Maybe it awoke my inner detective.

I ran my hand along the wood-panelled walls, scanning them for the Green Man as I went. I retraced my steps to the corner where Sophia's portrait hung, and then, *aha!* There in the panelling right above it was a Green Man wearing the very same moony grin. I put an X beside his box, and I looked up again. But something seemed different. Had the Green Man's tongue been sticking out like that before?

I checked the picture in the pamphlet. Definitely not sticking out there. Had I got the wrong Green Man? But I was certain his lips had been closed just a moment before. I thought it must be my empty stomach making me loopy. But just to make sure, I reached up with one finger and touched his wooden nose. What happened next was the strangest thing that had ever happened to me.

4

THE GREEN MAN'S SECRET

*W*hat happened when I touched the Green Man made me jump backward. The panel of wood on which both he was carved and Sophia's portrait hung made the quietest creek and opened inward on an invisible hinge. I had heard of trap doors in old houses before — things like that are always turning up in mystery novels — but I never expected to discover one! I looked about, one way and then the other. There was no one in sight. I shrugged, then ducked down and stepped through the door.

I was in a small chamber with no other door than the one I'd come through. But there was one small window, more like an arrow slit, and a pale beam of light seeped through, catching centuries of ancient dust in its stream. The light glinted off the only other object in the sparse room — a rusty old chest — and lit up a single painting that covered a large portion of the wall to my right.

Something about that painting drew me in. The colours were so rich and real; it looked almost like a photograph rather than a painting. It was the landscape of Otterly Park with the Manor rising up in the background, and away in the distant hills was a tiny hunting party. A grove of trees grew near a river in the foreground, and under the trees was a wagon, like the shepherd's huts I'd seen at some of the country fairs Nan and Pop took us to. A man in a flat, floppy cloth cap sat outside the wagon, smoking a pipe and dabbing paint onto a canvas, while a young girl with strawberry-coloured hair like mine watched over his shoulder. It was such a nice scene and made me feel a funny sort of hungry feeling in my stomach that wasn't my appetite. It was longing to be a part of that picture, to have *that* girl's adventurous life. What more could anyone wish for? The painter and the girl had a big, black horse for company and a lovely, smoking fire.

In fact …

I took a step back and blinked. Then stepped closer and squinted. *I really need to get my eyes checked*, I thought. The painting looked so real, I could swear that smoke rings were actually rising up from the embers! I stood glued to the spot, my eyes squinting then opening then squinting again. But as much as I squinted and glared, the smoke rings did not stop rising. My heart began to pound a little harder, and my eyes grew wider, transfixed by the rings circling upwards. Did I hear the faint sound of crackling flame, or was I imagining that too?

Then, like getting caught up in a whirlwind, several things happened at once. There was a creak and a slam. I whirled around to see the door of the secret chamber slam shut behind me. In a panic, I turned back to the painting. Thank goodness! It had stopped moving … or so I thought until, ever so subtly, the gypsy painter's face turned towards mine; the fire's smouldering embers lit up his dark eyes, and then, though I hardly believed my own senses, he winked! Before I could scream, run or faint, or any mixture of the three, I fell forward as if my whole body were being pulled straight into the painting!

You know that feeling you get when you're nearly asleep and you think you're falling? That's a bit what it felt like falling into the painting, only there was no jolt to wake me up. The dream just kept going. I kept falling through a swirling blur of colours spilling into each other. There was a loud whistling in my ears, like the sound of traffic whooshing past an open car window. At some point, the pull released me, and, for one instant, I was in free fall all on my own. The next second there was a flash of light. I felt wet, papery fingers whip across my face. Then, *thud!* Cold, hard ground came up to meet me.

I couldn't open my eyes at first. My head was spinning, like I'd just been tumbled about by ocean breakers. I wasn't sure which way was up and which was down. I just lay there, catching my breath. The chirping of birds told me I was outside. Sun rays lit up my closed eyelids, and I felt dampness of morning dew making my hair stick to my face.

When at last I thought I could move again, I propped myself up on my elbows, wiped the wet strands of hair out of my eyes and slowly opened one lid then the other. Staring back at me, just inches away, was a pair of big, brown eyes and a wet snout. The doe kept a watchful eye on me, but carried right on munching her mouthful of grass.

When I got to my knees, spitting out a mouthful of bracken, the doe froze, then darted off into the undergrowth, just in time for me to feel the *boom boom* of galloping feet approaching from behind.

WOOF!

I swung around just in time to close my eyes again before a shoe-sized, dripping wet tongue slurped across my face.

A girl's voice rang out somewhere in the distance. "BRITANNIA! TO ME!"

The enormous grey dog — biggest I'd ever seen — obeyed immediately, turning on its long, gangly legs and galloping off towards the voice. That gave me a chance to wipe my slobbered face on my sleeve and get to my feet.

But the sun was so bright by now, I couldn't make out who had called the dog. And where was I? I tried to get my bearings, but the park looked so different somehow. Yes, there was the front of the house, but where had all the cars gone? And where I thought we'd sat for our picnic earlier, there was a patch of dense forest. What was going on with my head? Had Nan managed to mix up those bottles of ginger beer with Pop's strong ale? I shaded my eyes to try and see the person approaching me through the wet grass and bracken. Perhaps she would be able to help me sort out where I was and how to get back to Nan and Pop.

The figure walked steadily towards me — a small woman in a great big gown. But as she got closer, I realised it wasn't a woman but a girl, probably not much older than me from the look of her plump, rosy cheeks. She was a solid-looking girl, and very pretty, I thought, feeling just a tinge jealous of her golden hair that beamed in the sun's rays.

The huge dog was at her side. Her pointed ears nearly reached the girl's chin which stuck out the top of a high, lace collar. The very sight of it made me scratch my neck without thinking, but it did make a nice frame for her flushed face and her golden hair which was woven around her head in braids like a basket.

As she got closer, there was no mistaking her for a girl no older than twelve or thirteen, though her eyes looked like they belonged to someone older. Those eyes were familiar. I almost felt as though I'd met her before … somewhere.

She was still too far off to call out to her, but I could make out her costume. It was so fancy and grown up! A beige silk gown with green embroidery climbing up the bodice like vines. The long cuffs on the sleeves matched her lace collar. But as beautiful as the dress was, it did look quite uncomfortable, like the clothes in all those stuffy portraits I had seen in the Great Hall.

That was it! This girl had to be a historical re-enactor, paid to dress up and act as if she lived in Otterly Manor's old days to make tourists feel like they've really travelled back in time! Of course, that made perfect sense. We'd been to medieval re-enactments at castles before, with jesters and jousting knights. Maybe this girl was dressed up like someone from the days of Queen Elizabeth or King Henry VIII. I'd seen costumes like hers in my history book at school.

The funny thing is, though she was just an actor, I felt the urge to curtsey when the girl stopped in front of me.

She was just right for the part, like a little princess with her sweet smile and her blue eyes sparkling. But I just stood there, feeling rather soggy.

"I do hope she did not frighten you?" she asked with what sounded like a bit of a foreign accent. "She is still a big puppy and ever so excitable." She held a scolding finger up to the dog. "But you must learn your manners, Tannia, or you shan't have any friends."

The "puppy" licked its drooping jowls, closed its lion-sized jaws and sat down obediently.

"It's ok. She didn't frighten me." I was alarmed to hear my voice quavering after my tumble. "I love dogs." To distract from my wet, slobbery appearance, I pulled off my backpack and took out Oscar's ball sling. "Does she play fetch?"

The girl cocked her head to one side. "Fetch?"

"I mean, will she chase a ball and bring it back to you?"

"Ah, I see! *Naturalich.*" The girl's eyes sparkled. "Yes, her breed is designed to retrieve fowl. But she doesn't do it much. I claimed her for a *Kammerhunde.*"

"I'm sorry, a what?"

"Oh, my apologies. It is German for *chamber dog*. I chose Tannia from her litter to be my companion. She was a gift from my Papa when I came to live here."

"That's a nice gift," I said, still a little confused whether she was acting or if the dog really did belong to her. "I wish my dad would get me a dog."

She cocked her head again, still smiling but with a slightly confused expression.

"Oscar — that's my Nan and Pop's dog — loves his ball sling. Can I throw it for her and see if she likes it?"

"Oh please!" The girl clasped her hands. "I have never seen such a contraption. I should like to know how it works!"

I held the ball to Tannia's nose to let her sniff it, then flung it in a rainbow arc through the air. She was after it in a heartbeat and brought it back with a wagging bottom to drop it at my feet, eager for more.

The girl laughed a musical laugh and clapped her hands. "It is most extraordinary! Could I try?"

For all her lace and ruffles, the girl was surprisingly agile and got the hang of the ball sling in only a couple of tries. We laughed at Tannia's lanky legs and overgrown paws as she lumbered after the ball, and laughed again when she set it down in a pool of slobber on the girl's leather shoes.

At last she handed the ball sling back to me with a little curtsey. "I hope you do not think me impertinent, but where do you come from? I've never seen such a jigger as that ... er, *ball sling* did you call it? And your dress and speech are unlike anything I have encountered since I came to England, though I have not travelled much in the northern shires ..."

I was sure the girl really *could* guess at my accent, but she was acting her part so well, I decided to play along. "Oh I'm not English." She watched curiously as I opened my backpack to stuff the ball sling down among my books and journals. "That is, my mum is English, but I live in America. I'm just here on holiday visiting my grand-parents."

"*A-mer-i-ca.*" She sounded out each syllable slowly, then folded her hands over her highly decorated tummy.

"My tutors have wronged me. They say I am excelling at Geography, but this *America* I have never heard of."

"Well," I began, trying to keep as straight a face as she was managing throughout this game of make-believe, "it *is* quite far, across the ocean in fact."

Her eyes widened as if in true disbelief. "You mean you come from the New World?"

I shrugged and nodded. "Sure. The New World. What about you? Where did you live before you came to England?"

"I lived in Wolfenbüttel Castle. In Saxony." She must have noticed me biting my lip, because she added, "It is a German principality. And most beautiful. I had a very happy childhood with my three elder brothers there. But —" she lowered her eyes and began stroking Tannia's smooth, grey head—"a year ago, when I turned eleven, my mother and father sent my brother Frederick and me to live at Otterly Manor as the Earl's wards."

"Oh." She looked so sombre, I almost forgot we were playing a game. "But why did they send you away?"

"As a ward, Frederick is to be the Earl's heir and make a good, Protestant match here in England." She looked up with a determination in her eyes. "And when I am older, I shall go to Court to wait on my aunt the Queen."

"The Queen is your aunt? Wait, do you mean Queen Elizabeth?"

"Oh no. But didn't you hear?" She looked shocked. "Queen Elizabeth died in 1603, three years ago now! My aunt, Anne of Denmark is the Queen Consort, the wife of His Majesty King James." She looked at me with wonderment. "America must be *very* far indeed ... How *did* you come to Otterly Manor?"

"I came with my grandparents. They're National Trust members."

"Ah. *Natürlich.*" Now she was the one biting her lip. "Is that a guild of some kind?"

I laughed, but thinking it was probably time to cut the game short and find out just where Nan and Pop and the rest of the tourists had got to, I changed the subject. "We didn't know there was a re-enactment going on today. I should really go and find them. Nan's probably worried by now."

"Of course. But before you go, allow me to introduce myself. My name is Sophia Matilde Hedwig Brunswick-Lüneburg, but do please call me Sophia." She curtseyed so low this time, it looked like her legs melted right out from under her. "And I hope you will come again, er ..."

"Oh, it's Katherine. But you can just call me Katie if you like." My attempt at returning her graceful curtsey felt more like miming a wobbly scarecrow. Sophia didn't laugh, but only smiled a friendly smile at me, her round pink cheeks glowing in the sunlight.

"You're really are an excellent actress," I added as we turned towards the house.

She wrinkled her forehead. "An actress? I am not much of an actress, though I do enjoy the plays of Master William Shakespeare. You must have heard of him? He is a favourite of His Majesty's."

"Of course I've heard of him. We did *Midsummer Night's Dream* at my school last year."

"So then *you* are an actress?" she asked most seriously.

"Not really. I just played one of the fairy chorus members."

She seemed to be thinking very hard, and I wondered what I had said that could be so very confusing.

"Actually," she giggled, sounding for the first time like a girl of twelve rather than a proper little lady, "Frederick and I did sometimes put on the most absurd comedies for our parents." She sighed. "But no more." She smiled a little sadly. "One day I *shall* be an actress. When I become a duchess, I shall have to learn to act in a courtly manner *all* the time."

Sophia's performance was interrupted by a woman's shrill, metallic voice calling out from one of the house's countless windows. Tannia's ears pricked up as the woman screeched, "Sophia, make haste! Master Van Hoebeek is ready to make your portrait! He says the muse is upon him. For heaven's sake, make haste!"

Sophia set her jaw. "I am sorry, Katie. I am wanted inside, but I do hope you are soon reunited to your kinsmen. God speed!"

She picked up her skirts and made for the house, but as she did, a strange sensation came over me. Talking with the girl had felt very…real. Not like she was performing at all. Besides that, everywhere I looked, Otterly Manor was different from how it had been that morning. Sure, it was the same house in the same park. But the stones and windows of the house were brighter, newer. Smoke chugged from the chimney stacks. The road leading to the house wasn't paved; it was smooth dirt. And coming up the hill at that very moment was not a car, but an ornate carriage drawn by two white horses and driven by a stiff man in a white wig. There was most certainly no sign of a car park or picnic tables, and not another normally dressed person to be seen.

I whirled around looking for any sign of Nan and Pop and Oscar, any sign of normal life. How could I, an aspiring detective, have failed to notice the world around me had transformed? I turned back to call after the girl … *what had she said her name was? Sophia something something something?* Sophia. *That* had been the name of the girl in the painting. Then it clicked. She *was* the girl from the painting! It all came rushing back to me: the Green Man, the secret chamber, the landscape painting, the gypsy's wink. Falling.

With a wave of panic, I swallowed a huge gulp of air and couldn't even shout. My head was spinning like a carnival ride, but somehow I managed to pick up my feet and run after Sophia.

"Sophia!" I croaked.

She turned and waited for me to catch up with her.

Gasping, I asked, "What year did you say it was?"

She laughed merrily, like she thought I was the one playing a game now. "Why it is the year of our Lord Sixteen-Hundred and Six, of course."

I looked right into her truthful blue eyes, and I knew. This was no re-enactment. Somehow, without meaning to, when I'd fallen through that painting, I had fallen back in time. Somehow, my wish to be a part of that other girl's world, of *Sophia's* world, had come true. And what was more — the thought chilled me like cold water running down my spine — I had no idea how to get back to my own world again.

5

VAGABOND

"My goodness, are you well?" Sophia asked, reaching out for my arm as my legs collapsed beneath me like a flimsy folding chair's.

The world was spinning again, and it was all I could do to keep breathing, in and out, in and out. How could it be the year 1606? I needed to get help, to tell Sophia what had happened to me. But then, what if she didn't believe me? What if she picked up her many skirts and bolted to the house when I tried to explain what had happened? After all, *I* could hardly believe it. But here I was, and it was no good sitting in the wet grass wondering how I'd got here. There was only one thing to do: I had to try to explain to Sophia and hope she didn't run for it.

She listened with a very serious expression, and when I described the painting and the winking gypsy, her eyes became wide and she gasped. But still she didn't scoff. She just stood back a little, her eyes fluttering over my clothes and hair like I was making sense to her for the first time. When I finished, I waited for her to tell me I was insane, but to my amazement, she just cupped her cheeks in her hands and whispered, "Tom Tippery."

"What's that?" I wasn't sure if Tom Tippery was a person or an old-fashioned way of saying *good grief*, or *Pete's sake*.

She clasped her hands together beneath her chin as if praying. "Tom Tippery is a travelling mercenary painter. I used to visit him and his daughter Bessy at his wagon where they live. But lately Tom has served as an assistant to the artist Master Van Hoebeek who is here taking the family's portraits, and I've hardly seen him or Bessy since. Master Van Hoebeek keeps him so very busy."

"By wagon, do you mean a sort of shepherd's hut?" I was relieved Sophia hadn't taken off running, but I was beginning to wonder what all this had to do with my predicament.

She nodded. "You've seen it?"

I shook my head. "Only in the painting."

"Ah. Of course. It used to be that the wagon stood just under those trees, there." She pointed over my shoulder. "But it moved after Master Van Hoebeek arrived, and I've not been able to find it." She clenched her fists in front of her. "I should never have gone there. But I never thought … Still I knew I shouldn't have said so much! But they were so kind to me, and Tom so good a listener, and I—"

"Sophia!" The shrill voice rang out again, this time from an upper window.

I dropped down, hoping the bracken would conceal me.

"What in heaven are you doing out there? Get inside at once!"

I peeked at the window to see the woman's pinched face scowling out from under her maid's cap.

"I am coming, Nurse Joan!" Sophia stepped in front of me, shielding me behind a wall of fabric. "I must first have a word with Digby about my horse. Beg pardon of Master Van Hoebeek and his muse for keeping them!"

Once the pinched face retreated and the window slammed shut, Sophia turned and pulled me up by the arm. "Come, Katie. I'll explain Tom and the painting as soon as I can. We'll hide you in the stables for now. Once Master Van Hoebeek has finished for the day, we'll think of what to do next. It may be I can steal a word with Tom after my sitting. If your coming here truly is his doing, he must tell us what to do about it."

Sophia took her skirt in one hand and grabbed my hand with the other, and together we ran for the stables with Britannia bounding ahead of us.

THE STABLES I'd seen that morning with Pop and Oscar had become nothing more than a great big storehouse for garden tools and paint cans, closed off to the public by a wire fence. But now, as we neared the building's grand archway, my nostrils filled with the sweet perfume of hay and horse. The snorts, hen clucks and whinnies of a living barn sounded like sweet music to my ears. *This* at least was something familiar, and I felt a little of my terror from falling into the past melt away.

"It's beautiful!" I gasped, walking under the arched doorway and taking in lofty beams and tidy stalls and — *at last!* — dozens of the most gorgeous horses.

"Are you a rider yourself then?" Sophia asked.

"Yes. I mean …" I gulped. "I … used to ride quite a lot."

Several horses turned their heads as I followed Sophia across the cobblestone floor. A lanky boy leaned against the wall with his hat pulled over his eyes, his long legs stretched out in front of him and his arms crossed over his steadily rising-and-falling chest.

Sophia cleared her throat and said kindly but loudly, "Master Digby."

Nothing.

She turned to Britannia and, pointing to the boy, ordered, "Tannia, mount."

The dog padded over to his bench, reared up on her back legs, and planted her paws firmly on his shoulders before snatching the hat off his face. His uncovered eyes grew as big as moons with fright.

"Mercy! The devil's hound! It's found me out!" he sputtered, flailing his arms and legs helplessly under the enormous puppy's weight.

"Tannia, to me!" The dog padded back to her mistress and dropped the hat at her feet.

"Digby, this is Mistress Katherine. Katie, Master Digby."

"Master, Ha!" The boy, who looked around sixteen or so, crept along the wall and made a grab for his hat. "I ain't master of nothing nor nobody." With a yank he freed the hat from Tannia's teeth and stood triumphantly. "But I'm at your service all the same." He made a rather absurdly pompous bow before pulling it back down over his mass of straw hair.

Sophia ignored his sarcasm and went on. "I'm very sorry, Digby, there's no time to explain, but would you please see that my friend is comfortable here and that no one disturbs her until I return?"

"I am yours to command, me lady." Digby made another melodramatic bow, this time with a flourish of the hand.

Sophia shook her head. "Never mind Master Digby's antics. I'm sure he can be relied upon." She gave him a playful warning look, then took my hand in hers. "I must go at once before Nurse Joan comes after me with a switch, but I shall return to you at first opportunity!" And with a curtsey and a swish of skirts, she was gone.

When it was just me and Digby, he stood there rubbing his hand over his stubbly chin as if not sure what to make of me. "So … you're from …?"

"Oh." I felt suddenly self-conscious of how strange my blue jeans, t-shirt and tennis shoes must've looked to him. "It's a long story." Hoping to avoid having to make up an explanation on the spot, I asked, "Maybe could you introduce me to some of your horses?"

He sneered. "None of them's my horse. I just look after them. But I can introduce you all the same."

For the next hour, I almost completely forgot I was stranded in the wrong century. This place was heaven. The barn was the most beautiful I had ever seen, with golden light pouring down through the upper rafters and lighting up the haystacks, glinting off hanging rows of pristinely polished saddles and spurs. But best of all were the horses!

We stopped at stall after stall, Digby pointing out the particular features of the Spanish racing horses or the hefty Dutch draught horses. There was a row of handsome Scottish nags that served as the family's personal riding horses.

I felt the old hunger to ride growing monstrous within me. I hadn't forgotten Mum's orders to stay away from horses during the holiday … but then, surely it didn't count in 1606, did it? Technically, Mum hadn't said it yet, and wouldn't for another few hundred years. In fact, when I thought of it that way, in 1606, I hadn't fallen off Gypsy in the New England Equestrian Championship and spent a month in the hospital! And that thought gave me another idea. I raised my hand to my head and felt along the side of my scalp. It was still there. The long, bumpy scar beneath my hair had travelled back in time with me.

I dropped my hand to my side when Digby suddenly turned around before we'd reached the last stall.

"And there you have it, Mistress Katherine. 'Tis each and every one of the Earl's horses. Best kept in the land, make no mistake."

"What about that one?" I asked, gesturing to the final stall Digby had turned his back to. It was filled up with a giant black stallion. He was a head taller than the nag beside him, and his coat steamed in the summer heat. "Is he one of the family's riding horses too?"

"Ah him." Digby whistled and stepped hesitantly in front of the stall door, keeping a good distance between himself and the black giant. "That beast you see before you is called Vagabond, and he is the most notorious horse in all of England." He paused, apparently waiting for some amazed response.

I noticed this too late as I was distracted by a long gash

down the horse's neck. Digby carried on with his tale. "Belonged to a breeder who sold him to the King's guard. Said his own daughter rode him daily and never had the least trouble with him. It must have been a lie, for Vagabond gave the King's guard more trouble than any horse before him. No amount of whipping or lashing would tame this one."

My mouth dropped open. So *that's* where the scar came from. A lash. "But he probably just missed his home and the little girl who used to ride him. Lashing him would only make him worse!"

Digby only shrugged. "Tell that to the King's guard if you like! They would have shot him, but the Earl heard of it and brought him here. Thought he might prefer the hunt to guarding. But old Vagabond is no better here than he was at Court. It's a wonder the master doesn't have him destroyed. Nobody's daring enough to try to ride him, and he's not good for any labour." Although we were alone, Digby leaned in close and cupped his mouth. "They say he's possessed with a demon." Then leaning back, he shrugged. "I reckon he's just Irish bred."

Suspecting Digby was having a bit of fun with me, I forced my face to stay perfectly relaxed. "Why do they say that? What does he do that's so bad?"

"What does he do, she asks? I'll tell you. Besides throwing off every soldier that tried to ride him in the guard, he has a vengeance for any living creature that crosses him."

I crossed my arms over my chest. "What do you mean, *a vengeance*?"

Digby widened his eyes and lowered his voice as if to

tell a ghost story. "Well, for one thing, he has a nasty habit of pigeon crushing."

I sniggered.

"'Tis true!" His eyes were wide. "The King's own groom said to the master, 'Mind this one in the stable yard. He'll stow away his grain in his jaws for hours. Then, soon as he's in the yard, he'll spit it on the ground and wait as if for the pigeons to come and peck at it. Then, when the poor fowls are least suspecting, Vagabond raises a hoof and brings it down, *SPLAT!*'" Digby clapped his palms together, making me jump. "All that's left is bones and feathers ... and, you know, entrails."

I shuddered at the mental picture. But I also felt just a little indignation on Vagabond's behalf and turned away from Digby to prop my elbows against the horse's stall door. I looked up into one of his deep, black, intelligent eyes. We held each other's gaze for an instant, then his nostrils flared and a puff of hot air made me blink. I must've smelled very strange to him, covered in whiffs of the twenty-first century. "Are you sure those grooms weren't telling a story?"

Digby leaned against the stall door beside me and sneered. "I didn't believe it at first either, but now I've seen the menace with my own eyes. Vagabond is the devil in a horse's hide."

"I doubt that," I said, reaching a hand up to stroke Vagabond's nose. "I've heard of the devil dressing up like a snake, but never as a horse."

Digby threw his arm out and swatted my hand back. "I wouldn't if I were you. He's known to bite."

I drew back my hand, but the urge to touch that horse

stayed with me, like a magnet drawing me in. I know it sounds silly, but I felt as though we understood each other. I had lost Gypsy, and he had lost the girl who used to ride him. We both knew how much it hurt to be torn away from a best friend. As Digby led me away, I turned to look back over my shoulder and met Vagabond's still-watching eye.

6

NEW SHOES

I'm pretty sure my watch stopped working when I fell through the painting, but I heard a bell toll the hour twice before Sophia came back. After my tour of the stalls, I sat and chatted away with Digby. Luckily, he seemed much more interested in talking about himself than asking me questions. Though his mood was jolly enough, I got the feeling Digby wasn't quite content with his life as a stable hand at Otterly Manor.

"It seems like quite a nice place to work to me," I offered after a wave of ranting about his daily duties and pining for one morning's lie-in. "I'm hoping to work in a barn when I grow up."

He must've thought I was joking because a gusty laugh exploded through his lips. But he quickly became sober again. "It isn't the work I mind so much. It's not having what *they* have." He gestured towards the house-facing wall. "I can play the part of a courtier as well as any one of them! Why, it's easy!" He jumped up and performed a hilarious series of prances, bows and poses until I was holding my stomach laughing. "All I need's a pair of fine stockings and a ruff collar! I look almost the twin of Master Frederick, but," — he put on a very convincing German accent — "he will inherit Otterly Manor along with a title and a life of ease. And I? I will inherit only ..." he pointed to a pile of manure — "that."

After a while, Digby had to get back to work cleaning the stalls and watering the horses. I offered to help, secretly hoping for an excuse to sneak back to Vagabond's stall. But Digby said the idea of a "lady" cleaning stalls was unthinkable. I told him I wasn't a lady, just a girl, but it was no use. So I curled up on a sunlit pile of hay in the corner and read *The Hound of Baskervilles* until my eyes got droopy.

Just as I was drifting off, fast high-heeled footsteps startled me awake again.

At first I didn't recognise Sophia. She wore an even fancier blue velvet gown and her hair was all pinned back in a funny hat. But she smiled her same angelic smile when she saw me, and Tannia bounded over to lick my face again.

"Oh, Katherine! I have kept you so long. Tom Tippery was there for my portrait sitting, but when we had finished, Master Van Hoebeek called him away, and I wasn't able to speak to him! I am truly sorry. But—" she held out her arms which were full of fabric — "I did manage to find you some clothes." One by one, she showed me the plain white shift and apron, corn blue petticoat and brown shoes. "I hope you don't mind, but I thought we might best disguise you as my chambermaid. There is so much superstition among the servants, it is better they didn't see you in your *native* dress. It wouldn't do to have anyone spreading rumours that you are a witch."

My eyes must've gone wide, because she laid a consoling hand on my arm. "Don't worry. I shall help you fit in until we can speak to Tom about sending you home again. Now let's go up into the hayloft. No one will be up there, and I will be *your* dressing maid."

I was very much impressed by how Sophia managed to climb the ladder to the hayloft in all her skirts and ruffles as if she'd grown up in a barn. When we'd both reached the top, she showed me to a corner tucked away behind stacks of hay bales where I could change. Dozens of pigeons roosted in the pitched rafters above me. I changed as quickly as I could, feeling a little exposed with their beady eyes twitching with my every movement. First went on a pair of woollen stockings and the white, cotton shift that looked like an old-fashioned nightgown. Then the blue petticoat which had a dainty bit of flowery embroidery, though nothing as fancy as Sophia's dresses, and thankfully the skirt didn't poof out quite so much. I was sure I'd never be able to slip through doors as gracefully as Sophia with a hula hoop around my waist.

"Come out when you are ready, and I will help you with your laces and your apron," Sophia's muffled voice offered from the other side of the hay bales. The dress wasn't uncomfortable, but I wheezed involuntarily when she drew up the laces in the front, and then tied the apron on even tighter. Though she concentrated, I could tell she wanted to ask something. Finally, as she tied the laces into a double bow, she said, "You must be terribly frightened,

Katie. To be so far from home, I mean." Her big, blue eyes looked at me questioningly.

I thought about it for a moment. The funny truth was, I didn't *feel* terribly frightened, though I knew I *ought* to. "I don't know," I answered at last. "I guess it hasn't quite sunk in yet … I mean, I still feel like I'm in the middle of a very strange dream." Sophia nodded, and I said, "Can I ask *you* something?"

She took my hand. "But of course! Anything you wish."

"Why weren't you, well, more surprised when I told you where I'd come from? I mean, if someone turned up out of nowhere and told *me* they'd travelled from the future, I'd probably think they were a bit loony."

Sophia looked thoughtful. She sat down on a hay bale and began playing with a loose strand of hay. "I *was* surprised. I never thought such a thing could happen in God's earth! But …" — she looked up with worried eyes — "Oh, Katie, can you forgive me? I fear that I am partly to blame for bringing you here."

I stood frozen in my woollen stockings. "What do you mean? How could you have …"

"I did not mean to do it! You must believe me. I have prayed for a friend like you ever since I came here to Otterly Manor. The only person I ever told was Tom Tippery. *He* brought you here somehow; I don't know how, but it *had* to be him." She stood up and took my hand again, "But however it happened, I vow to you that I shall do everything in my power to return you to your rightful home as soon as may be. And, in the meantime, I hope you shall be very happy here."

She looked so hopeful that in spite of all the questions swirling around my brain, I smiled. "I think I will, as long as I can figure out how to walk in *those*." I pointed to the pair of leather, clog-like shoes with hard, little heels.

"They are my recreation shoes. I do hope they fit you." She eyed the pair of pink tennis shoes I'd tossed aside in a heap of my own, modern clothes. "I fear *those* would raise too much attention. My, but they *are* extraordinary!" As I struggled into the clogs, she carefully picked up one of my shoes and turned it in her hands as if she were examining a diamond.

"Try them on!" I said.

She looked scandalised, but quickly sat down, pulled off her own high heels and slipped her feet into my tennis shoes. "So comfortable!" she exclaimed, taking tiny, dainty steps.

The shoes looked so funny with her beautiful gown, I had to laugh out loud. "Oh, I wish I could take a picture of you!"

Sophia looked confused. "You mean a painting?"

"No, I mean a photograph. Oh — "I slapped my fore-head — "I forgot. Cameras don't exist yet."

"Your world must be so different! I should like to know all about it, but perhaps these are mysteries better left to the future. I am most curious to learn more about *you*, Katie, for though we may belong to different times, I feel that we are just alike!"

She was right. "I feel that way too," I said, standing up for the first time in the leather shoes. "And I want to learn more about *you*, but first I need some help learning to walk in these things." The shoes fit, but felt as stiff as wooden boxes.

"Try to walk across the loft," Sophia encouraged.

Hands out for balance, I took my first steps across the hay-covered floor only to topple over and land flat in a hay bale!

We both laughed so hard, it took a few minutes before Sophia was able to haul me up to my feet again. Once we finally brushed off all the bits of hay, Sophia stepped back to examine me. "You look a perfect lady in waiting now," she said, kindly ignoring my swaying back and forth. "A little more practice walking, and you will fool the entire household."

I smiled back, but the thought of trying to fool an entire household of adults from this strange, past world, who might just mistake me for a witch if I behaved out of the ordinary, made my insides go as wobbly as my legs.

7

THE CHAMBERMAID

S ophia's plan was to pretend that I was her new, foreign chambermaid (to explain my funny accent), recently sent by her father to keep her company. She seemed entirely confident this ruse would work, but I felt less certain. Would I be able to pull it off?

"Trust me, Katie. This household is so very large, no one will bother much about a new chambermaid. Although, perhaps 'tis best to stay clear of the Earl and Countess as you could not have been sent here without their knowledge."

"But won't it be difficult to avoid them?" I was trying to imitate Sophia's perfect posture and confident walk. "I mean, it is their house after all."

"Not at all!" She dismissed the worry with a wave of her hand. "The Earl is oft away at Court or in Oxford, and I rarely see the Countess except at meals. But then you shall dine with the household in the Great Hall, so you needn't worry."

After a few more practice walks up and down the

stable carriageway, I said goodbye to Digby, thankful he was too preoccupied filling stalls with fresh hay to pay any attention to our charades. It was time to brave the household and kick off my acting career as a chambermaid. I followed as close as a shadow behind Sophia under the tower gateway and across the grass courtyard, then through the second gateway and across the stone courtyard. When we reached the entrance to the Great Hall, she looked about and whispered to me, "Remember, you belong here, Katie. If you believe it, no one will doubt you."

I nodded and held my head a little higher as we stepped across the threshold.

I could hardly believe the house we entered was the same I'd seen that morning! The Great Hall echoed with the murmurs and bustling feet of servants going about their chores. Where the hall had been empty that morning, now there were three long tables with benches. Sophia popped her head into the buttery to have a word with one of the maids. Meanwhile, I stood gawking at the transformation of the place. The whole room looked as if a wind had blown through and taken the dust of years away with it. The walls were a cheery bright yellow instead of faded, and every brass knob and wooden carving gleamed with fresh polish. Like a wish come true, a fire crackled in the enormous hearth. The room felt so much cosier, and smelled so much nicer, like fresh paint and plaster instead of must and mildew.

At the end of the long tables, we turned into the passage that led to the Great Staircase. I liked the tapping sound my hard shoes made against the wooden stairs, and

I smiled at the familiar heraldic leopard who now wore a fresh, vibrant coat of paint.

The long, narrow portrait gallery was just as wonky as I remembered it, but it was friendlier now with the sun coming in from the far window and Tannia's toenails tickling the floorboards behind us. The portraits gave me that same eerie feeling of watching, only this time I felt they knew my secret that I didn't really belong here at all. A second later, I discovered that theirs were not the only eyes boring into me.

A woman marched towards us from the far end of the gallery carrying a basin and a towel. I recognised her pinched, frowning face as the one that had been poking out of the window earlier. *Sour* was the word that sprang to mind. Her withered lips gave the impression she'd been sucking on a lemon for the last fifty years. Her beady eyes narrowed in on me, and with each step closer, her frown went further south until it was a full-on grimace.

"Mistress Sophia, *who* might I ask is *that* creature accompanying you?" She held me with her hawk-eyed stare, like she was ready to snatch me in her talons should I try to scamper away.

"You may indeed, Nurse Joan." Sophia was as cool as a cucumber. "This is my new chambermaid and companion, Katherine." Then she turned to me. "Katherine, this is my nurse maid, Nurse Joan, who has so kindly tended to me ever since I came here to Otterly Manor."

Nurse Joan hardly waited for Sophia to finish before snapping, "Katherine, you say? *Just* Katherine?"

Sophia prompted me with a nod.

I cleared my throat. "No ... no it's ... Watson." Charlie's nickname for me had come to me in that moment of need, so I didn't stop to question it. "Katherine Watson." Watson isn't actually my surname, so I suppose if I'd wanted to be technical about it, I had told Nurse Joan a lie. But after all, I was in disguise, pretending to be an old-fashioned chambermaid, so I might just as well pretend to be a chambermaid called Watson. And anyway, I thought, what would Charlie say if I broke the first rule of going undercover and gave the suspicious old bird my *real* last name.

"Watson?" Nurse Joan was not appeased. "What is your parentage, girl?"

"My parentage?" I glanced over at Sophia who was still nodding encouragingly. "Oh, you mean, like, my parents? Of course." I cleared my throat again, trying to think up more important sounding names for Dad and Mum. "My parents are ... erm ... Lord Peter and Lady Jemima ... Watson. They're not from around here, so you probably won't have heard of them." I hoped to goodness she couldn't hear how loudly my heart was pounding. I've never had much talent for telling lies.

"No, I should think not." Nurse Joan stepped closer so that she practically loomed over me. I could feel the breath from her nostrils against my bangs. "You are clearly of foreign extraction. Who sent you here, and why was I not informed?"

Sophia stepped between the old woman and me, her face set with determination. "God sent her, Nurse Joan. She is an angel."

Nurse Joan's thin mouth twisted in disgust. She

53

propped one bony hand on her waist, hugging the basin with the other arm. "An angel with red hair, Mistress?"

Sophia gracefully folded her hands. "In my country, the great masters *always* paint angelic beings with red hair."

"Well in *this* country, we call it devil-kissed," Nurse Joan hissed. Her eyes flashed at me like warning lights, making me gulp.

Sophia didn't flinch, but remained perfectly matter-of-fact. "My aunt, the Queen of England, has red hair. I shall tell her next I see her that Nurse Joan suspects she has been kissing the devil."

At that, Nurse Joan went paler than pale and nearly dropped her basin. "That is not ... not what I meant," she stammered. "To be sure, red hair is a mark of beauty. I would not dream of—"

"I'm sure we all say things we don't mean at times." Sophia smiled graciously at the stricken old woman. "I shall forget all about it, Nurse Joan. That will be all, thank you. Katherine is weary from her journey." And with a graceful nod to Nurse Joan, Sophia pulled me away.

Grown-ups are always calling me *precocious* because I read hard books and use big words for my age, but Sophia's wit was as quick as a hare, and I had to admire how coolly she used it. Nurse Joan still stood frozen to the spot when we turned the corner at the end of the portrait gallery, arm in arm. Sophia waited until we were in a closed room, well out of earshot, then turned to face me. "I thought you did very well, Katie. You mustn't let Nurse Joan trouble you. She is a meddlesome, superstitious old lady, and far too possessive of me. But she means well, I'm sure." She set her hand on a shiny brass doorknob. "Would like you to see my bedchamber? And yours, of course, for as long as you are here."

"Yes, please!" I already felt much steadier than I had a moment before, and I forgot all about Nurse Joan when we entered the most amazing bedroom I had ever set foot in.

It was just like something out of Cinderella's castle! Every surface was covered in fabric fit for a queen: tapestries with minstrels and scenes of lovers covered the panelled walls; there was a giant-sized four-poster bed hung with heavy, red velvet curtains, a Turkish rug to warm the wooden floor, and a velvet cushioned settee in front of the glowing hearth (although it was summer, that draughty old house needed every fire lit). Tannia immediately flopped on her side and made herself comfortable in front of the blaze. I was tempted to follow her example.

"Would you like some powder?" Sophia stood at the dressing table with an opened silver pot in one hand and a brush in the other. "Perhaps we should make you look a little more up to date, don't you think?"

"Don't you mean *back* to date?" I joked.

Sophia laughed. "*Natürlich*! I suppose I do. Now close your eyes tightly." With a stiff brush, she dabbed my face with a chalky white powder, then rubbed some wet pink stuff on my cheeks. "There. What do you think?"

I bent over to peer into the silver mirror and snorted. "I look like a jester!"

We put on more of the ridiculous powders, rouges and lip paint until we were both laughing so hard that tears clumped the powder on our cheeks.

I straightened up when a maid came in carrying a tray of tea things.

"Thank you, Tatty," Sophia said, gripping her sides.

The maid didn't say a word, but looked at my streaky face like she'd seen a ghost. She set down the tray, made a hurried curtsey and dashed out of the room. That only set us off laughing again. I don't think I've ever laughed so hard with anyone except Charlie. And all that giggling worked up my already raging appetite.

"Oh I love English afternoon tea!" I said as we sat down at a little table in the sunny window alcove.

"Afternoon tea, do you call it?" Sophia looked bemused. "We only call it dinner, though we did drink tea when the Portuguese emissary came to stay."

"You mean you don't drink tea normally?" That came as a shock. "But what do you drink then?" I asked. If I couldn't count on the English to know about tea, how was I to survive in this strange time?

"Beer or wine mostly." Sophia handed me a tiny crystal glass with some yellowish liquid in it. "Here. Try some."

I took a mouse-sized sip and nearly gagged. It was so bitter! But I forced myself to swallow and smiled politely. Luckily the table was laid out with other recognisable dishes like soup, bread, meats and cheeses to comfort me in the absence of tea.

Sophia took a sip from her glass. "The beer is made here at the manor's brewery, though we make much better in Germany."

I raised my own glass to my lips, pretended to sip, then set it down again. "You must miss a lot of things about your home."

"I miss my mama and papa, and my older brothers, Otto and Leopold. People think my papa stern, but at home he is full of laughter. We all were in the old days, when we were all together."

"It seems a shame they had to send you away," I said. "Don't you find it miserable and just so … unfair?"

Sophia set down her spoon and looked thoughtful. "I suppose nothing is fair when you look at it the wrong way. You might say it is not fair that I was born into a noble family when so many are born poor. Or, from the other direction, you could say it is not fair that common children oft get to live with their families when I must be sent away to live with strangers."

I nibbled a bit of bread, trying to imagine how my situation could ever look *fair* from another direction.

Sophia took another sip from her cup and put it down with a thoughtful look. "My mother always told me, 'Sophia, each of God's creatures must take the lot given him and make something more of it.' Like the parable of the tenants in the gospels. The good servants are those who take the coins their master gives them, and multiply them two, even ten-fold. The wicked servant is the one who buries his coins in the earth and makes nothing of it, then gripes about his situation."

I squirmed a little in my seat, remembering what Mum had said about making the most of my situation. But making the most of things certainly didn't come to me as easily as it seemed to come to Sophia. I was amazed by her. How could she just accept things the way they were, even when that meant leaving her home forever?

With an expression as earnest as a philosopher's, she

carried on. "It isn't miserable to do one's duty for the sake of her family. By coming to England, preparing for a life at Court, I bring good to those I most love. Besides, there is so much to learn and enjoy here. Although," — she turned her thoughtful gaze towards the window — "I confess, life here can be lonely at times, especially now Frederick is away at Oxford."

Hearing Sophia at least admit to feeling lonely made me feel a little better about myself. I was beginning to think she really was as perfect as her painted portrait.

She turned her glowing cheeks back from the window. "But I can hardly complain. I have Britannia, and now the Lord has sent me you!" Her smile fell suddenly into a frown. "But how very selfish I am to speak of my home when *you* are the one truly far from home. And how you must long to return to it. Tonight you must tell me more of your home … Of your family … What your times are like. And tomorrow Master Van Hoebeek is sure to call me to pose for him. You can sit with me and steal a word with Tom Tippery about getting you back there."

"I'll tell you about where I come from if you like. But actually," — I leaned back in my chair and popped a juicy grape into my mouth — "I'm not in *too* much hurry to get back. Things are pretty rotten at home just now. So I'm lucky to have met you, really."

Over the next hours, I tried and failed to describe what the future was like to Sophia, things like cars (carriages that move without horses was the best I could do) and television (portraits that move and act out plays). And although she could hardly understand what I was on about, we laughed like the oldest friends.

The maids came and cleared away the dinner things and tended the fire. Then Sophia showed me a journal in which she sketched birds that she observed in the park, and I showed her some of my own drawings from my spy notebook. Though she wouldn't admit it, hers were better by miles! People often compliment me on my artwork, but Sophia's sketches were better than any twelve-year-old's I'd ever seen.

Then she showed me a screen she was stitching with a Bible passage bordered with lots of little pictures. It was so detailed, I said it must've taken years to do, but she insisted it was easy as anything and gave me a lesson in stitching. I was just getting the hang of it when a maid knocked at the door to announce it was time for Sophia's lute lesson.

"Oh I am sorry to leave you alone when you've only just arrived, Katie. Do make yourself quite at home while I am detained. I shan't be more than an hour."

"It's alright," I assured her. "I'll keep practising my stitches. Hopefully I'll have got them down by the time you get back." I did practise the stitching, just as I'd said I would … for about five minutes. But without Sophia there to talk to, the room had fallen ghostly quiet, and I started feeling a bit jittery. I looked over the beautiful objects on the dressing table, put my nose into a bowl of spicy potpourri and tried to decipher the stories sewn in the tapestries. The minutes seemed to be dragging their heels. I looked at my watch, then remembered it had stopped working since I'd fallen through the painting.

The painting …

There had been so much newness to take in, it hadn't

occurred to me before now that the magic painting I'd fallen through that morning *must* be in the house somewhere. What would I find if I visited the secret cupboard now? Did the household even know the cupboard existed? Maybe it was Tom Tippery's secret, right under the Earl's nose.

Though I wasn't overly eager to jump back into the modern day world *just* yet, I felt it would be more pleasant to know for certain that a way home existed ... when the time came that I wanted it. Besides, curiosity about the cupboard was becoming so strong, I thought I might burst if I didn't at least try to have a look into it.

THERE WAS no one in the portrait gallery when I poked my head around the corner. I tried to tip-toe in my hard, high-heeled shoes, but the floorboards still squeaked relentlessly! I kept reminding myself that I wasn't doing anything wrong walking down the corridor. After all, I was a guest in this house. And yet, being caught could lead to uncomfortable questions, and the thought of meeting Nurse Joan's hawk eyes around a corner made the hairs on my arms stand up.

But I made it down the corridor without a single eye spotting me — except those belonging to the nosy old portraits — then turned right into a window-lit passage that looked down into the stone courtyard. A serving woman carrying a pail in each hand and a man with an armful of firewood crossed each other's paths; but there was no sign of Nurse Joan below, thankfully. The larger Billiard Gallery was just as quiet and empty as the corridor, *and* there was hay threshing on the floor, which helped to muffle my footsteps. I made my way to the far corner of the gallery, ready to face that fateful Green Man once again.

The Green Man was there, tongue tucked politely away in his cheek; but in place of Sophia's portrait was that of Mr. Fancy Pants that had been in the Great Hall that morning. And now that it was close-up, he looked even more ridiculous than I remembered. Everything about him curled: his eyebrows curled, the tips of his moustache curled, the ribbons on his shoes and doublet curled, and one corner of his arrogant mouth curled in a kind of snarly grin. What Charlie would make of this absurd character! For the second time, the thought made me snort with laughter.

"Pray, what amuses you so, my lady?"

I choked on my own laughter and spun around. The deep voice that had come out of nowhere belonged to a tall, straight man standing right behind me. How he had sneaked up so close without my hearing, I will never know!

"Nothing!" I said in a voice that belonged to a five-year-old. "I was just thinking of a joke I heard ... once."

"Oh?" He looked at me with dark, piercing eyes, and I realised with a twist in my tummy that he was waiting for me to tell him the joke!

In hot-faced desperation, I pretended to study the portrait.

"Do you know this gentleman?" the tall man asked in what I now recognised was some sort of European accent. He certainly looked foreign with his chin-length straight, brown hair that stuck out from beneath his hat, and his thick, black beard that looked just like sheep's wool.

"No. I ... I don't know him," I answered. I didn't care for the way he glared at me down his long nose. I just hoped he wouldn't follow up his question by asking who I was. I had a name handy, but I hadn't taken the time to come up with a believable history just yet.

Thankfully, he was much more interested in the portrait than in me. "That is the Earl's youngest brother, the noble Baron of Chudleigh. It is one of my proudest accomplishments."

"Oh, you painted it?" I squeaked. Though I'm tall for my age, I felt suddenly very small caught between the snooty gaze of the man in the painting and the hard stare of the black-bearded man.

"It doesn't belong here, a masterpiece like this." He spoke right over my head, as if to the painting and not to me. His dark eyes scanned over it like a man looking at his love. "But soon enough ... soon enough it shall be restored to its place of glory in the Great Hall."

I swallowed more loudly than I'd meant to, and his eyes focused back on me with a look of suspicion. "I believe *you* do not belong here either? Shouldn't you be waiting on your mistress?" He stood so close, I had to scrunch up my neck and forehead to look up at him. I felt just like a tortoise pulling its head up inside its shell.

"Sophia, that is, *my mistress*, has gone to her lessons. I was just ... admiring the paintings." I had the sudden fear that if I took a step backward, the panel behind me might just swing open and give away my secret. I stood as stiff as a wood panel myself, still craning up at the man frowning down at me.

The corners of his woolly moustache turned up, though his eyes stayed cold. "Your taste does you credit. Allow me to introduce myself. I am the Master Painter Van Hoebeek, commissioned to portray this household as befits them." He gave a slight bow with his head. "And you must be Mistress Sophia's maid?"

I cleared my throat. "Watson. Katherine Watson." I made an awkward curtsey as I could hardly move.

I felt warm relief melt over me when Sophia's bell-like voice called from the other end of the gallery. "Katherine, are you in there?"

Like a spell snapping, Master Van Hoebeek stepped aside and I could breathe again.

"My Lady." This time, as Sophia approached, the painter made a low bow so that his silky straight hair made a fringe curtain right over his face.

Sophia smiled politely but looked unimpressed. "Master Van Hoebeek." She curtseyed and turned back to me. "I am sorry to have kept you so long, Katie. Master Fiorelli was most passionate about today's piece. Shall we go and dress for supper?" She curtseyed once again to Master Van Hoebeek, then linked her arm through mine.

I had the prickly feeling that Master Van Hoebeek was watching us make our way down the gallery, but when I chanced a glance over my shoulder, he had vanished as silently as he'd appeared.

8

A ROYAL ANNOUNCEMENT

*A*lthough I was meant to be a chambermaid, Nurse Joan and another younger maid came to help Sophia into her supper gown and do up her hair in what looked to me like a fishing net. Thankfully, Nurse Joan appeared to be pretending I didn't exist. I was happy so long as she didn't look at me with those piercing eyes.

When Sophia was washed and dressed and all pinned up, she looked at me, tapping her finger against her cheek. "And what about you, Katie? Your hair is a little short for combs or nets."

She was right about that. When Sophia's blonde hair was let down, it hung in one long curtain right down to the small of her back. My strawberry-coloured hair was straight and fine. It used to be long, but a lot of it had to be cut off for surgery after my accident. It had grown back fast enough, but still only just brushed the tops of my shoulders. There wasn't much anyone could do with hair like mine.

"Aha!" Sophia said, struck with an idea. She ran to her

dressing table and came back with the fanciest headband I'd ever seen, covered in light blue ribbon and pearls. "There," she said, fixing it on top of my head. "Now you are ready for the Great Hall."

SOPHIA HAD her supper with the Countess and important guests like Master Van Hoebeek in a room called the Great Chamber which was in part of the house near the family's private rooms. I was to have my supper in the Great Hall with the rest of the household servants. That was part of Sophia's cleverly devised plan in making me a chamber-maid, so that I could escape the notice of the Earl and Countess.

It was rather nerve-wracking going down that Grand Staircase all by myself. I stepped into the Great Hall, now softly lit with summer twilight and flickering firelight, and truly alive with a hundred or more servants. The sight of all those people gave me a knot in my stomach that reminded me of my first day at middle school, walking into the cafeteria and looking wildly around for a familiar face while trying to appear like I knew where I was going.

To my relief, and the relief of the knot in my stomach, I did spot a familiar face. Digby sat at the near end of the closest long table with the table cloth stuffed down his shirt and a drumstick in one fist. I waited for him to finish speaking to the man beside him, then approached. There was a seat on the bench in front of him, and I hoped he just might invite me to sit there.

"Hello again, Digby," I said, trying to sound chirpy and confident.

"Greetings, Mistress Katie." Digby turned to the man at his side and said, "Jack, this is Katherine, Mistress Sophia's new chambermaid and companion."

"Jack Hornsby." The man tipped his shaggy brown head and smiled pleasantly. "Second Groom."

"You work in the stables as well?" I asked, with genuine chirpiness. "I'd love to hear more about the Earl's horses." I decided to take my chance. "Is anyone sitting here?"

Digby threw his head back and guffawed. "Mistress Katie, your place isn't with a couple of lowly stable hands likes us. 'Tis at the High Table," — he gave his head a toss towards it — "with other important personages like yourself."

"Oh …" Once again, I wasn't entirely sure whether Digby was being serious or pulling my leg. The important thing was not to let the two men see how clueless I really was. "But, aren't I a servant too?"

"Yes, but not all servants are created equal, now are we?" Digby answered with a sarcastic note in his voice. "You're one of the waiting servants. That makes you cream of the crop along with the steward and the dressing ladies and our chief groom. Off you go, up to your seat of honour!"

I didn't feel particularly honoured being sent away like that; but I walked away with my head held high, as I imagined Sophia would do, and stepped up onto the platform (which I'd learned that morning was called a dais, just like the ones kings and queens sit on) to take an empty seat at the High Table.

Nobody greeted me or even smiled at me when I sat,

but a couple of teenage maids peered over at me and whispered to one another. A skinny arm appeared over my shoulder, and I glanced up to see a serving girl putting some sort of pie on my plate.

"Thank you," I said, but she said nothing and moved on to the next seat. I noticed then that her clothes were quite a bit plainer than what I and the other girls at High Table had on. The serving girl's dress looked like coarse wool or cotton and was cut in plain, straight lines. Mine was made of a finer, stiffer sort of stuff, and though my skirt didn't poof like Sophia's, it certainly had more flounce than the serving girl's. Clothes, it seemed, were a sort of code language here, and one I would have to learn to read very quickly if I was to fit in without notice.

I didn't mind so much that no one spoke to me. It was certainly better than stirring up more suspicion! But I did begin to feel self-conscious after several minutes sitting there staring down at my plate. Luckily, my apron had pockets, and by a stroke of good luck, I'd put my little leather-bound *The Hound of the Baskervilles* in one. I reached under the table, slipped it out and spent the rest of supper holding open the book with my left hand whilst shovelling bites of hot pie with my right. The book provided a nice sort of shield from curious looks, and I could glance over the page without being quite so obvious.

That morning on the tour with Nan and Pop, there had been a chart on the wall showing the different members of the household staff. I decided to make a game of guessing who was who at the High Table. I thought the two whispering girls must be the Countess's waiting ladies. The finely dressed, portly man with a wig and an enormous nose *had* to be the head steward. And after him … I nearly choked on the bit of pie in my mouth when I caught the eye of Nurse Joan sat at his side, her wiry frame nearly hidden by his barrel of a belly. She had obviously been giving me a sideways glare which she quickly tried to cover up when I caught her. I too tried to make myself look less suspicious by pretending to be examining the paintings on the wall behind the High Table. I had just decided the middle one — an austere looking man with a long white beard — must be the Earl, when another wigged man came positively bounding up the dais. He scurried around to the other side of the table like he hadn't a second to lose and placed a sealed letter in the steward's hand.

I watched as the portly gentleman flicked it open, held a funny little pair of spectacles over his eyes and hastily scanned the page. Though it was hard to tell through his thick layer of powder, I could swear his face went whiter and his eyes swelled like balloons. He threw the cloth from his shirt and stood up, knocking the table with his big belly so that the cups rattled and every eye turned to watch him.

He gathered himself for a breath or two, then bent down and whispered into the ear of a lady, who in turn looked amazed and whispered to a gentleman on her other side. The steward marched out of the room and disappeared into the Great Staircase chamber, but the chain of whispers continued, right down the length of the High Table.

And it didn't stop there. Soon the entire Great Hall was a hushed murmur of excitement. But strain as I might, I could not make out what any of the murmur was about!

I was beginning to wish I had made a little more effort to speak to the servants at High Table as at least one of them might have passed the secret on to me. I turned in my seat to take in the commotion in the hall behind and saw that Digby and the Second Groom were just getting up from the table, locked in conversation.

"Digby!" I swished over as quickly as I could without tripping over my skirt. Digby and Jack turned and waited for me. "Is everything alright?"

Digby ran his fingers through his wild straw hair and blew out a whistle. "Depends on what you mean by *alright*. Nobody's died, but some of us may be driven to our graves by the morrow!"

Jack nodded in agreement.

"Why? What's going on?" I asked, anxious to hear what horrible calamity was coming to Otterly Manor *on the morrow* as Digby put it.

My anxiety must've shown on my face, because Digby took one look at me and snorted. "Don't worry yourself. It's no mishap for *you* lot. All you must do is see that the Mistress is dressed in her finest. Meanwhile, *we* lot will be breaking our backs whilst the Earl and family put on their pageantry."

I was properly confused by then. "What pageantry? You mean the Earl's coming home? That's what this fuss is all about?"

"Well no, that's not the whole of the matter, is it?" He elbowed Jack, then put on his *air of confidentiality* again. "It's like this, Mistress Katie. The steward's just had a letter from the Earl. Says he's riding home post-haste on the morrow *because* he's just received word direct from the Royal Court that His Majesty has changed the course of his Summer Tour. So the King will now sojourn at Otterly Manor starting from two days hence. It seems His Highness wants a look at the Earl's refurbishments on his grandfather King Henry's old place." Digby and Jack were both shaking their heads in bitter disbelief, the way Nan and Pop do when complaining about the weather.

"Wait." I was trying very hard to boil down Digby's explanation. "The King is coming here? In only two days?" His language was so funny, I wanted to be entirely sure I'd got the message right.

"Not just the King. The entire Court is coming here in two days," Digby corrected, waving his hands for emphasis. "Well Jack, we'd best begin readying the stalls. There'll be no respite for the likes of us till the King and his royal equines depart."

Jack and Digby walked away, deep in conversation about the work that awaited them, and I found myself the only one standing still in a swirling sea of bustling bodies. With the news of the King's coming, the Hall had become like an agitated beehive, and my head was buzzing from the excited chatter. I slipped out into the Great Staircase chamber without anyone noticing and climbed the stairs as quickly as I could. This day had been nothing but mad, and I needed somewhere quiet just to think and be.

When I crept into the red bedchamber, Sophia was already there. The two dressing maids were helping her out of her supper gown and into her nightgown.

"Have you heard the news, Katie?"

I thought for the first time Sophia sounded more like an excited twelve-year-old than a prim and polite lady.

"About the King? Yes. Just now." I tried to match her excitement.

"Do you know what this means?" Freeing her hair from its net, the maids released her, and she skipped across the carpet to take my hands.

I thought for a second, then shook my head. "Well, no. Not really. What *does* it mean?"

"It means," her blue eyes sparkled, "the Earl is riding home from Oxford on the morrow to oversee the preparations for His Majesty, and Frederick shall ride with him! He is coming home at last, and the two of you shall meet!" She was so happy, she skipped me around in a circle before the fire that crackled merrily as laughter.

After I'd slipped into one of Sophia's spare nightgowns and we'd washed our faces in the basin, we climbed into the giant canopy bed. I nestled down under the weight of the covers and laid my head on the downy pillow. Sophia's long blonde locks fanned out over her pillow, and she was smiling so broadly, her rosy cheeks looked like two red apples.

We chatted happily for a while, Sophia describing her brother to me and all the fun we would have in the coming days. I listened, but at the same time I thought how strange it was that I'd only just arrived in this other world earlier that very day. Sophia treated me as if I belonged here. As if we'd be friends forever. As if she almost forgot I lived in a world hundreds of years away.

As if she read my thoughts, she became silent, then rolled over on her side to look me in the eye. "It is so nice to have a friend with whom I can share this happiness ... you don't mind being here for a while, do you, Katie?"

"Of course not! I'm having a wonderful time!" I said, pillowing my cheek in my hand. "I mean, everything is still a bit ... new. But honestly, this is the best summer holiday I've ever had."

She smiled, then her face turned to concern. "But I am sure you miss your family. Just as I miss mine. On the morrow, we shall speak to Tom. But I am glad you will stay long enough to meet Frederick first. He will love meeting you and hearing about the world you come from!" Sophia rolled over to her other side and blew out her candle. "God bid you fair dreams and peaceful sleep, Katie. I am glad you are come."

"At home, we say 'goodnight, sleep tight, don't let the bedbugs bite'," I responded, and we both giggled. After a few minutes, I heard Sophia's steady breathing and turned over to watch my own candle flicker and throw shapes on the wall. All the talk of Frederick had made me think of Charlie. I wondered what he was doing in Scotland, and whether he missed me and wished I had come along. That's when it hit me, like a stone on water: *Charlie doesn't exist here. None of them do.*

The thought made me shiver in spite of the weight of warm covers. I propped myself up to blow out the candle, then lay back, shutting my eyes tight against the dark. When I woke, would I find this whole strange day had been a bizarre dream? Or was my adventure at Otterly Manor only just beginning?

9

THE BLANK CANVAS

*W*arm sun rays lit up the insides of my eyelids. I opened them. A stream of silver morning light poured through the open bed curtain and landed in a pool on my pillow. I stretched, yawned and sprang up like a jack-in-the-box. I found myself inside a cosy cocoon of crimson. Outside the red curtains, I heard the hushed voices of ladies and the soft scuttle of a dog's claws on floorboards.

So it wasn't a dream.

I scooted across the bed to the open curtain and dangled my legs over the side. Sunlight bathed the bedchamber; it sparkled off the silver objects on the dressing table and left a latticed design across the floor. Odd, I thought, that all the paintings from back in these days should look so dark and creepy. This morning was fresh and dazzling … and delicious! A whiff of something savoury tickled my nostrils, and my eyes followed my nose to a steaming tray of bowls and platters on the table.

I planted my feet on the thick, Turkish rug and looked

about the room. Sophia was sitting by the fire, already dressed and with Britannia chomping a deer antler at her feet. One of the maids was combing Sophia's hair back and fixing it into a complicated bun.

"Is that you, Katie?" Sophia asked, unable to turn around.

I padded across the carpet to stand beside her at the fire. "You look very nice!"

"Thank you. I would sooner wear fewer petticoats, but Master Van Hoebeek has requested an early portrait sitting as the Earl is due to arrive by midday. I was just going to wake you."

"How long have we got?" I asked, squatting to stroke Tannia's boxy head.

"Oh time enough for you to dress and for our breakfast. I only had to make an early start as this hairstyle does take an age for poor Tatty to perform."

Tatty did look rather taxed, I thought, with pins stuck between her teeth, and her eyebrows pinched in stern concentration as she wrestled Sophia's long, golden strands.

"Shall I call for Elinor to help you dress?" Sophia asked.

I was going to say I could manage. Then I remembered the ordeal of lacing and latching my dress the day before and decided to take her up on the help. So Elinor came and had it all done up in no time, and I was dressed and seated at the breakfast table before Sophia's hair was even ready. Tatty finished her off with the lacy ruff collar that stood straight out, a bit like those plastic cones dogs wear when they've got an injury they mustn't lick. I was thankful I didn't have to wear a stiff, scratchy thing like that!

We had to go to the drawing room for the portrait sitting. Master Van Hoebeek greeted Sophia with what must have been a very tickly kiss on the hand through his woolly black beard.

She turned to me. "Katie, I believe you met our resident artist yesterday?"

Master Van Hoebeek, as expressionless as one of his portraits, bowed his head towards me.

"And *that* over there is his apprentice, Tom Tippery."

I hadn't even noticed the other man sitting in a shadowy corner behind his easel. He too had a beard, but it was short and scraggly and salted with white. It was easy to tell who was the Master and who was the assistant. Unlike Master Van Hoebeek's fine, silk clothes, Tom's were plain and woollen and looked like they needed a wash. He stood and doffed his flat, floppy cap in a bow, revealing a large bald patch. When he raised his head, he looked me right in the eye and gave me the slyest wink, and I knew with a skip of my heartbeat, it was him. *He* was the gypsy painter I'd seen in the painting. *He* was the one who had brought me here, somehow or other.

I was dying to ask how and why he'd performed his magic on me from centuries away, but my questions would have to wait. It was straight to business before Master Van Hoebeek's *artistic muse* could run away. A bird cage stood near Sophia's stool, and she took from it a dainty, yellow canary that perched and chirped happily on her finger. The artist positioned her on the stool and ordered Britannia to lie down beside her. Britannia cocked her head but didn't budge. Sophia ordered her, "To me, Tannia," and the dog trotted right over and obediently lay down beside the stool.

I sat myself down out of the way in a hard, wooden chair to watch and wait. The morning passed more slowly than the longest car journey I have ever suffered through. It must have been hours! I will never know how Sophia sat there, still as a marble statue, for so very long. To keep my eyes from closing, I watched Master Van Hoebeek at his work. Though I couldn't see much from the opposite side of the canvas, it was still quite a performance. Sometimes his brush strokes became quite violent, slashing across the wooden canvas. Other times, he dabbed delicately like he was tickling it. Tom Tippery, meanwhile, sat in his corner and appeared to be doing very little other than plodding away with his own paintbrush.

How I wished I'd brought my book along! I had constantly to shift around in my chair to keep from nodding off. After what felt like half a day (though it was probably no more than two hours), Master Van Hoebeek *finally* put down his paintbrush. Leaning back, he observed his work and rubbed his hands together.

"It is nearly finished," he said in his wiry accent. "And, if I may be so bold, a work of rare beauty."

"May we see it?" Sophia asked. Our plan was that she would find a way of distracting Master Van Hoebeek while I tried to steal "a private word" with Tom Tippery.

The painter smiled wryly. "I'm afraid I cannot reveal it to you until I have applied some … final touches."

It was a good attempt, but it hadn't worked.

Sophia didn't miss a beat before trying the next strategy. "Master Van Hoebeek, I wonder ..." She hesitated just long enough to cast a meaningful sideways look at me. I straightened up, waiting for my moment. She continued, "I have always imagined having my portrait taken in the park, with my horse. My aunt, the Queen, has one such portrait in our gallery. Have you seen it?"

"Yes, I believe I know the one," Master Van Hoebeek answered with only half of his attention. The other half was employed in packing away his brushes.

Sophia boldly jumped up and walked over to the window, the canary still bobbing on her finger. "I've found just the perfect backdrop. I believe you can see it from this window. But I should like your expertise, if you'd care to have a look?"

This time, Sophia's ingenious plan paid off. We shared the sneakiest of smiles as Master Van Hoebeek made his way across the room to her side. Here was my chance! I crept along the wall and stopped just behind Tom Tippery's easel. He was still busy adding his own finishing touches to his canvas and didn't seem to notice me.

There was no time to lose, so I cleared my throat. "Hello, Mr. Tippery. I'm Kat—" Before I could even get my name out of my mouth, the strangest thing happened. Tom jumped to his feet, nearly knocking over his easel. He looked at me with wide, terrified eyes as if I were a ghost. Pushing me aside, he flew to Master Van Hoebeek's stool and threw a cloth over the painter's canvas before snatching it up under his arm. But he hadn't been quick enough in covering it to hide a rather interesting feature of Master Van Hoebeek's painting. *It was blank!* After hours of slashing, dotting and tinting, there was not a spot of paint to show for it!

I was speechless. Tom and I stood there gawking at each other, he clutching the blank canvas under his arm, his eyes darting between me and the window. Master Van Hoebeek must have heard the clamour and turned around. When he saw Tom and me in our face-off, his eyes narrowed angrily on me for half an instant, then softened. "Is anything … amiss, Tom?" he asked with nonchalance.

Sophia looked at me questioningly.

Tom opened his mouth as if to answer, but he only just managed to mumble, "Er, no … sir."

The drawing room door opened, and the moment of pins and needles was shattered. We all turned our attention to the man servant who stood as stiff as a soldier in the doorway.

"The Earl has arrived and requests the audience of Mistress Sophia and Master Van Hoebeek at dinner," he announced.

Sophia gave a little jump for joy, then caught herself and looked at me, biting her lip. I'm sure she didn't know what to make of my befuddled face. "Master Van Hoebeek," she asked as innocently as a little child as she returned the canary to its perch, "Would you be so kind as to escort me to my guardian?"

Master Van Hoebeek cast one last dark glance at me, then straightened up. "But of course, my lady."

"I will meet you after dinner, Katie," Sophia called over her shoulder as she took Master Van Hoebeek's arm. "How about in the Stone Court? It is such a fine day, we can go for a walk."

I nodded and waved awkwardly as she left, then spun around to seize the moment with Tom Tippery. My jaw dropped. The man was gone! Completely vanished without a peep! And Master Van Hoebeek's blank canvas had gone with him. He had, however, left his own canvas and painting kit in the corner. I moved around it, half-expecting to find another blank board. But to my astonished eyes, what I found instead was the most exquisite likeness of Sophia! It was the one I'd seen in Otterly Manor that morning, almost complete.

So Tom wasn't just an apprentice; he was the *real* artist! But if that was so, what was Master Van Hoebeek? Why would Tom allow him to steal all the credit for his own work?

I rubbed my forehead, trying to make sense of it all. My stomach made a complaining gurgle, and I decided it was no good trying to solve a mystery until I'd had some lunch. Then I could tell Sophia all about what I'd seen, and perhaps she or even the famous Frederick would have some answers.

But as for speaking to Mr. Tom Tippery, it wasn't going to be as simple as I'd imagined. I was just going to have to wait a little longer and watch a little closer.

10

SNEEZING SUSPICION

I waited for Sophia in the Stone Court on a sunny bench, reading my book. I'd nearly finished it and had just got to the part when Holmes and Watson are lying in wait in the fog-veiled mire only to be sprung upon by a giant, fire-breathing hound!

"Katie!"

I jumped at the sound of my name.

Sophia and I met each other's surprised faces and both laughed. "*Phew!* I was just getting to the scary bit," I explained, tucking the book back into my apron pocket.

"Well I hope you shall find us less frightening." She stepped aside to present a tall, sinewy boy with the same serious blue eyes, flushed cheeks and wavy blonde hair as her own. He was quite dashing with a neatly trimmed, golden goatee. I thought he might have been around Charlie's age.

"Frederick, *this* is my new friend I have been telling you about, Katherine Watson."

"Mistress Watson." Frederick smiled and made a very

gentlemanly bow. It made my face burn to hear him call me by my code name so very politely. Charlie would die laughing if he'd heard it.

"Sophia tells me that you are from the Americas, but she will not tell me how you came here." He spoke in the same slight German accent as his sister, and had the same look of genuine interest in his eyes as he spoke. "She says I must ask you to tell me yourself."

"Oh, erm, well …" I began, not really knowing where to begin. "It's a funny story, really …"

"Wait." Sophia laid a hand on my arm. "The manor is crawling with ears. Everyone is bustling about preparing for the King and Queen's arrival. We should go somewhere quieter where we can talk without being heard."

"Is it a secret? Is this Katherine Watson a fugitive? Or perhaps a foreign spy?" Frederick teased.

"Even better!" Sophia stuck up her nose with pretend snootiness. "Now where shall we go?"

"How about the stables?" Frederick suggested. "Or better yet, the hayloft? 'Tis a good place for thinking … or divulging secrets." He wiggled his eyebrows.

"But Frederick, what about your hay fever?" Sophia asked in her motherly way.

He looked affronted. "What hay fever?"

FREDERICK SNEEZED for the tenth time, just as I'd finished explaining my fall through the painting.

"Come now," he said through watery eyes. "You girls are practically ladies and much too old for these fanciful

81

children's games. Where have you *really* come from, Katherine?"

At Sophia's prompting, I had just given the whole strange account of the previous day's incident, and to my extreme discomfort, Frederick wasn't buying a word of it. He had an unamused look on his face that made my cheeks go hot, like he thought I was just a silly little girl.

Sophia stood up so that she was taller than her brother who sat on a bale of hay. "'Tis not a game," she said defiantly. "We can prove it." She looked at me to produce the proof.

"Yes!" I said, wishing Sophia had simply let me make up some believable story to tell Frederick. "I can answer questions about the future ..." I was quite good at history, but just then, I was scrambling to think of any historic fact that would impress him. He didn't even give me the chance.

"That doesn't prove anything. You could just make it up." He crossed his arms and leaned back against the curved wooden rib of the stable's vaulted roof.

I bit my lip, trying to think of something ... anything to show I wasn't being childish. If only I had a mobile phone or a tablet to knock his stockings off with. But I hadn't come with any modern technology. Even my watch was useless. All I had to show from the future were books, but that gave me an idea. "I know! I've got this." I took the copy of *The Hound of the Baskervilles* from my pocket and handed it to him.

Sophia nodded triumphantly. "Yes, have a look at that! The sketches are most strange and otherworldly."

Frederick took the book with a smirk and flipped

through its pages, stopping to examine the illustrations. He looked especially closely at the inside cover. His smirk turned into a perplexed scowl. "Who is this *Sherlock Holmes*?"

"He's a detective," I answered. "Probably the most famous detective in all of English literature."

Frederick scanned the page with eyebrows knitting all the while, like he was trying to solve a puzzle. "It says 'originally serialised in 1901'." He smirked. "I suppose you want me to believe that you have come here from nearly three hundred years in the future?"

"Not exactly."

"No?"

This wasn't going as I'd hoped. I sighed and launched into my explanation. "That book is an antique. It was a gift from my brother Charlie because we both love detective stories so much." How I wished Charlie were here! He'd know how to persuade Frederick, who was still scowling at me. "Anyway," I continued, "the Sherlock Holmes mysteries were written about a hundred and fifteen years before my time. I'm from the twenty-first century."

He closed the book with a thud and flatly handed it back to me.

Sophia was smiling. "So you see, Frederick. Now you believe us, don't you?"

Frederick kept glaring at me like he was trying to see into my thoughts. I sat as still as stone and dug my hands down into the hay beneath me. I was determined not to show Frederick any of the signs of dishonesty I was certain he was looking for.

"Sophia," — he addressed his sister but kept his eyes

fixed on me — "I have read of such intrigues as bodies transported through time. I do not advise tampering with games that may have ... devilish origins."

I nearly swallowed my tongue at that. Thankfully, Sophia came to my defence.

"Devilish? In truth, Frederick, is not God the Master of Time and not the devil? Do you not remember the verse Mama embroidered on your handkerchief before we left home?"

"Of course I remember." He took a cloth from his pocket and read the tiny thread words embroidered on it. "But as for me, I trust in You, O LORD, I say, 'You are my God. My times are in Your hand."

"You see?" said Sophia. "Time is in the *Lord's* hand. Only he could have turned it back."

Stuffing the handkerchief back into his pocket, Frederick jumped eagerly into debate mode. "Yes, of course. The devil's servants cannot *actually* travel through time. But they might use trickery or witchcraft to make us believe they had."

Sophia was not daunted. She crossed her arms over her chest and answered, "Since just when are you so quick to believe in old wives' tales? Is that what they teach you at Oxford? And what is more, when have *I* ever been known to tell a lie?"

I tried to back her up, but my own voice came out as shrill as a piglet's squeal. "I'm not a witch, I promise!" I squeaked. It was so unfair of Frederick to accuse me of trickery when *I* was the one who'd been tricked into going back in time. "I didn't mean to fall through that painting," I insisted. "It was an accident!"

"Frederick, I cannot believe you would be so discourteous as to accuse my friend of consorting with the devil! And anyway, Katie is only here because *I* asked for her."

I looked at Sophia, completely surprised.

"You did?" Frederick and I asked at the exact same time.

"Yes. 'Tis true." Sophia sat down beside Frederick and looked earnestly into his eyes. "I became lonely after you went away to Oxford, So Tannia and I took to exploring. That's how we met Tom, the gypsy painter, and his daughter Bessy. I sat beside his fire and listened to tales of their travels across England. Wonderful tales! And then Tom told me I had been so kind a listener, he would paint for me whatever my heart most desired, and it might even come true. I told him that what my heart most desired was for God to send me a true friend at Otterly Manor, for I would be better able to do my duty here if I had someone I could talk to."

Frederick's scowl softened and he placed an understanding hand on his sister's shoulder. "And then?"

"When I went back to visit Tom and Bessy again, their wagon had moved. The fire had all turned to ash. That was before I knew Tom had come to work as Master Van Hoebeek's apprentice. But he left me a note tied to a tree saying I should watch carefully for the friend I'd prayed for." Her blue eyes sparkled at me. "And only two days later, Tannia found you, Katie, lost in the bracken! So you see, God *did* answer my prayer, and Katie was his answer, so she surely can't be the work of the devil." Sophia finished and gave her brother a defiant nod.

Frederick looked sternly at his sister and then at me.

But soon his face relaxed and he took his sister's hand in his own two.

"I know you have been lonely here, Sophia. And I am glad you've found a friend." He smiled *almost* warmly at me. "But as your brother, I must still caution you not to spend your time unattended with strange gypsy painters, or to give much heed to what such people say. Though I do confess, I'm of half a mind to ask Tom Tippery to paint me an answered prayer of my own." He yanked out his handkerchief and sneezed into it once more.

Sophia and I exchanged a look. All the brotherly protectiveness and accusation seemed to drain out of Frederick. He had bigger fish frying in his mind than worrying about where I'd come from — *all the better for me*. He drooped over, bracing his elbows on his knees and his chin on his fists.

Now it was Sophia's turn to show concern. "But Frederick, why? What is it your heart is desiring?"

"A different lot in life." He stood up and paced the hayloft's small patch of floor. "The university has taught me much, Sophia. Philosophy. Theology. Things that matter. But I want more than a good education, just bits of knowledge I can flaunt about at Court like a jester's tricks. I want to *do* something … *important.* Like Papa."

"You mean you want to be a rector like Papa and further the Reformation?"

His face lit up. "*Genau!* You understand! There's so much I want to do … to write pamphlets, help translate the Greek scriptures into modern languages, reform the corrupt legal systems across Europe … "

"But Frederick, your place is in England now. Papa

sent you not just to study, but to represent our family and our faith in this country. It is a noble task."

I watched the passionate battle between the two flush-faced, bright-eyed siblings wondering who would come out on top.

"Noble?" Frederick plopped back down, sinking into his bale of hay as if the word had shot him down. "Nobility is all a game, Sophia. And I don't have the appetite to play it when there are *truly* noble tasks afoot."

Sophia crossed her hands in her lap and addressed Frederick just like a little mother. "But have you forgotten? Papa is both a rector *and* a prince. *You* can be both a rector and a nobleman. And think of the great influence you will wield in Court when you are an Earl! You could even become a university chancellor like Lord Buckville and teach Theology to England's brightest young men!"

Frederick crossed his arms and gazed up at the swallows darting between the vaulted rafters. "*Nein,* Sophia. What I long for is the life of an itinerant teacher, free from the chains of courtly duties. All this coquetry and banqueting is a foolish waste of time."

Then, so suddenly it made me start, Frederick jumped to his feet and stood in front of me. "Enough of me. Mistress Katherine, I do not pretend to believe or understand your story. But you have been a true friend to my sister in my absence and for that you have my thanks. Whatever secrets you have, you may keep them if you wish." He held out his hand to me. I stood and placed my hand limply in his, not quite sure how to take being thanked and called a liar in one breath. He gave it a squeeze and bowed.

"Thank you," I said, making an awkward curtsey as I tried to pull my skirt apart from the hay bale. And just like that, the tension was broken.

Frederick wiggled his nose. "I think I've had enough of hay. What shall we do now?" He turned to his sister. "Or do I detain you from your lessons, *Kleine Schwester*?"

Sophia was shaking the hay out her skirts. "Lessons are cancelled for the day in light of preparations for the King and Queen. But the Countess has asked the Dancing Master to hold a special session for us this afternoon, to be sure we are ready for the banquet.

Frederick groaned. "And the pageantry begins!"

"Don't make such a fuss," Sophia scolded. "You can be a gentleman and ask Katie to be your dancing partner."

My ears pricked up hopefully. "You mean I can come?" I'd taken ballet when I was younger and had always loved dancing, but I never dreamt I would be allowed to attend the ball.

"*Natürlich!* You are my lady in waiting! And anyway, the dance masters often snatch grooms or maids from their duties to serve as our dancing partners. Digby is always volunteering. He is an excellent dancer. Surprisingly light on his toes, for a boy who works with horses!"

At that moment, we both noticed a strange look enter Frederick's eyes, like an idea had just possessed him. A smile flickered on his lips, and he clasped his hands together.

"What is it, Frederick? You are making your mischievous face."

"Digby!" he answered. "Digby is just the man to whom I wish to speak."

11

THE SWAP

*W*e spotted Digby before he spotted us, whistling to himself as he shovelled out stalls in the stables below. Between every few scoops, he would stand his pitchfork upright and skip around it like it was a maypole.

"You were quite right, Sophia!" Frederick said, laughing out loud which made Digby jump a foot in the air. "Our good stable boy is as light on his feet as a maiden!"

Poor Digby hid his scarlet face by hastily doffing his cloth cap and bowing low. When he rose up, he wore a broad smile that turned his dusty cheeks to cherry tomatoes.

"Master Frederick, welcome home! I've just been attending your horse."

"Oh?" Frederick jumped down from the last few rungs of the ladder. "It looked to me as though you were attending your fair dancing partner." He pantomimed a bow to Digby's pitchfork. "She is the thinnest maid that 'ere I laid eyes on. Does she eat well?"

Though Digby still looked sheepish, he shared the laugh with Frederick, and Sophia and I, reaching the ground in turn, joined in. The two boys clasped one another's arms and dived into conversation about university life in Oxford.

I wasn't listening. A beautiful chestnut stallion in the nearest stall caught my eye, and I found myself thinking about Vagabond, wishing I could break away just for a moment to see him by myself. Sophia must've noticed my fascination with the horse.

"He's called Zues," she said. "Would you like to meet him?"

I nodded. "I'd love to."

We climbed up on a wooden crate to greet Zues.

My heart did a little skip as I reached out and felt the horse's warm neck. It couldn't help thinking that this was the first time I'd touched a horse since the accident. *It's ok,* I told myself while trying to force back images of that horrible day. *Don't panic. Don't be a baby in front of everyone.*

I don't think Sophia noticed that I was shaking. She seemed to be thinking of something else. "Frederick is lucky, you know," she said, calmly stroking the horse's velvet nose. "He and Digby struck up a friendship ever since the first days we came here. In fact, we often jest that the two are brothers separated at birth. Just look how similar they are!"

I dropped my hand from Zues's neck and released the breath I'd been holding as I turned around to have a look. Now Sophia pointed it out, she certainly was right. Once I looked past the obvious difference in clothing, the boys looked amazingly similar. Both were tall and lanky, though strong-looking. Digby's hair hung a bit longer and shaggier than Frederick's; but it was the same golden yellow, like sunlit hay. Also Digby's features were softer and not so solid and manly as Frederick's German ones. But even so, they could easily pass for brothers … maybe even twins.

"Actually, Digby, I've a proposition for you," Frederick was saying. "How would you like to attend the royal banquet on the morrow?"

Sophia spun around in alarm. "Frederick!"

I looked from Sophia to Digby. His jaw hung open and a sort of hungry look lit up his dazzled eyes. Becoming suddenly self-conscious, he threw his head back and laughed. "Now there's a lark, Master Frederick! Me? A nobody? At the King's banquet? What, and dance with the noble ladies in my stable breeches and jerkin?" He pulled at the baggy legs of his brown, woollen knee breeches. "Or shall I bring my pitchfork for a dancing partner? Ha!" He pitched another fork full of hay into the stall, speaking over his shoulder. "You're a right jester you are, Master Frederick."

But Frederick wasn't laughing. "Don't be absurd, Digby. Of course you shall wear my finest doublet and silk breeches. And if you don't mind, you shall also bear my name throughout the evening as well. You see, I'd sooner spend the night out here with your pitchfork than in a hall full of noble ladies myself."

Digby had stopped pitching hay again and stood there dumbly. I could see in Sophia's intense blue eyes that she, on the other hand, had been holding her tongue as long as she possibly could.

With her fists on her hips and her chin in the air, she snapped, "Have they been teaching you the art of deception at Oxford, Frederick? How do you hope to reform the Church and become a great rector if you break the commandments and bear false witness?"

I looked at Frederick who was avoiding her glare by taking a turn stroking Zeus's nose. "And have you not been telling your share of stories, *Schwester*?"

That made Sophia's cheeks flush with anger. I felt pretty irritated too that Frederick *still* thought we were lying or playing childish games, but I thought it best to leave this fight between brother and sister and moved away to stand beside Digby.

"At any rate," Frederick continued, "I am not a rector yet. Nor shall I ever be if I commit to a life of flattering His Royal Highness."

Sophia opened her mouth to speak, but Frederick jumped in too quickly. "Besides, you said yourself our friend Digby was an excellent dancer. It would be an ungodly shame if he never got the chance to use his skill." He crept an arm around Sophia's shoulder, but she stayed as stiff as a pin. "Come, *Schwester*. Consider, it will only be one night."

Sophia jumped off the box, leaving her brother's arm to drop by his side. "And what if Digby is recognised? He will be thrown into prison for dressing above station, all thanks to you and *your* ruse! If Father were here, he would remind you of your duty to be a good steward of the opportunities given to you, and be thankful for them." She swung around and looked Digby squarely in the eye so that he hung his head. "And that goes for you too. There is no shame in being a stable boy if you do your task unto the Lord with dignity."

Frederick stepped between them and took the pitchfork from Digby's hand. "Then we shall do one another's tasks with dignity." He smiled down at Sophia, but she turned her face away. "All will be well, *Kleine Schwester.* Let us not ruin our precious time together with quarrelling."

"Only be for one night." Digby chimed meekly.

I remained a fly on the wall. Frederick's plan didn't seem *so* bad to me as Sophia seemed to think it; but then, there was so much about this century I still didn't understand. And I wasn't about to take Frederick's side over Sophia's when she'd defended me so valiantly.

After a moment's hot silence, Sophia took my arm. "Come, Katie." She spoke to me as if Frederick and Digby had vanished from our presence. "We have a dance lesson to attend."

PREPARATIONS

*H*ow I wished that dance lessons could have carried on all day! My ballet lessons came in *very* handy. Though Sophia knew the dances already and performed them to perfection, the others were impressed with how quickly I picked them up.

I blushed when even the Dancing Master said so everyone could hear, "Exemplary poise, mademoiselle. Like a graceful doe!"

Sophia remained stiff towards Frederick and Digby; but even she couldn't help laughing with the rest of us when Digby followed the Master too closely, and the feather in his cap went right up Digby's nostril and made him sneeze so loudly the poor man screamed like a woman. Only the Dancing Master wasn't doubled over with laughter.

After the lesson, we spent the rest of the day trying to stay out of the way of the preparations. We walked in the park, sat in the garden and drew birds, and Frederick gave me a lesson in billiards which I thought was a more like croquet on a table than modern-day pool.

I said goodbye to Sophia and Frederick when it was time for supper, and made my way downstairs alone. The air felt tense in the Great Hall that night. It reminded me of the nerve-wracking moments waiting my turn to ride at a horse show, going over every jump in my head and wishing it could all be over. I suppose for the household staff at Otterly Manor, hosting the King must have felt like a performance as well, and they all wanted to receive top marks for their parts.

It was a relief to get back to the cosy red bedchamber and warm my feet in front of the fire with Sophia and Britannia. We talked about the banquet while sipping from tankards of hot milk and honey.

"Frederick is being very foolish," she said with a sigh. "Everyone in my family is stubborn and headstrong, but I think perhaps he is the worst."

"I can be quite stubborn sometimes too," I admitted. "Even when I know I'm wrong. My mum says I could out-kick a mule." Sophia giggled. "Who knows?" I shrugged. "Maybe he'll change his mind tomorrow. And if he doesn't, well, I guess at least Digby will have his chance to be a nobleman for a night."

"Yes." Sophia's eyebrows were furrowed. "Maybe then he'll finally see that spending his day with horses is actually quite nice compared to the company of some courtiers."

I laughed. "Are they very snooty?" I asked.

Sophia gave me a mischievous look out of the corner of her eye. "Well let's just say, the Dancing Master is not the only one who lacks a sense of humour when being sneezed at."

After emptying our tankards, we twirled away the evening in our nightgowns, practising our dance steps on the Turkish rug. At last we danced ourselves to bed, eager, and a little nervous, for the next day to arrive.

THE MORNING WAS NORMAL ENOUGH. The first item before breakfast was choosing gowns for the banquet. Sophia showed me her top three, and I chose a green one with gold ribbon for her. The sleeves were embroidered with roses. It looked just the sort of gown a storybook princess might wear, especially when Sophia's golden hair fell across the green silk.

Sophia was too kind to feel really jealous of her, but I did wonder just a little how it would feel to have such beautiful hair and wear gowns like that.

She laid the green gown on the bed and took another one from the pile. She held it up in front of me and wrinkled her forehead thoughtfully. It was a beautiful yellow velvet, the colour of her canary bird, with puffy sleeves and little yellow gems down the front.

"What do you think?" she asked.

"It's very lovely. Reminds me of Belle from *Beauty in the Beast*."

"Who?"

"Oh, she's just a make believe princess from a fairy tale."

"Well I think it is perfect for you." She held the gown against my shoulders to check its length.

"For me? But shouldn't I dress like the other servants?"

"There will be so many people in the Great Hall, and so many new faces among all the courtiers, the Earl and Countess will not think you out of place. And besides, you must dance! You are so good at it!"

The thought of dancing in that yellow gown in front of the King and Queen of England sent a million nervous little ants running through my veins. I had to clench my jaw to keep my teeth from chattering. "I hope I don't mess up!"

"You will be exquisite. Remember?" She imitated the Dancing Master's snooty, flamboyant air and French accent. "You 'ave exemplary poise, mademoiselle'."

We floated on a cloud of nerves and excitement right through breakfast, giggling at the slightest thing.

The rest of the morning passed in an ordinary way. We were to go to church in the town. Luckily for me, the Earl and Countess were staying behind to oversee preparations for the banquet, so I got to ride in the carriage with Sophia and Frederick.

As we made our way to the carriage through the manor, I felt just like I'd shrunk and gone inside a swarming hive. The whole huge house buzzed with anticipation. Maids flung linens out of windows and beat them with racquets. Clangings and shouts erupted from the buttery. Even out in the park, dozens of men were pitching tents, and others carried ropes of quails. I looked away when two men crossed our path with a dead deer hanging from a pole and quickly climbed into the carriage before any more dead things crossed our path.

The church looked just like the old stone parish church

my grandparents attended. Without thinking, I glanced over at to their usual pew when we entered, half expecting to see them there ... then remembered. I had been so preoccupied, I'd almost managed to forget my family didn't exist. Sitting through the long service, away from all the buzz and excitement, a hollow feeling began to grow in my stomach until it swallowed the nervous butterflies that had been fluttering there all morning.

"Are you well, Katie?" Sophia asked as we climbed back into the carriage.

"Oh, yeah," I smiled. "I was just thinking of my family. This church reminds me of the one my grandparents go to, not far from here."

She patted my hand with her gloved one and smiled sympathetically. "I was thinking, you know. Tonight Master Van Hoebeek will be occupied among the courtiers. It may be the perfect time to speak with Tom Tippery. I'll help you find him as soon as I can escape without being missed."

"Thank you," I said. And I meant it. I was enjoying every minute of my adventure, but I would enjoy it so much more if I knew when and how I'd be getting back home again.

13

A ROYAL WELCOME

J first laid eyes on the Earl and Countess just before the arrival of the Royal Court. I had a good view of them where they stood in the gatehouse carriageway. All the household servants that could be spared, along with the Earl and his family, lined up in front of the house to greet the King and his procession. The Earl looked a very solemn man with his black scholarly gown and long, white beard. The Countess was much younger, but she too looked no-nonsense in a heavy, brown gown and boxy hat. She was boxy all over, actually, and as stout as a pony.

When at last the King's Court arrived, it was like watching the Macy's Thanksgiving Day Parade in New York City, only with horses, carriages and canopies in place of floats, balloons and convertibles. Up they came through the leafy park, carriage after carriage pulled by some of the most handsome horses I have ever seen. When the footmen opened the carriage doors, we all strained our necks to see what manner of plumes, frills and laces would emerge next. The courtiers made a fascinating fashion show as they passed under the gatehouse arches, bowing and curtseying to the Earl and Countess.

After so many bows and curtseys that I thought the poor Earl's knees would give out (he did look about a hundred), a carriage unlike any before it appeared on the hill, and everyone gasped. It was covered in gold, from its hanging tassels to its wheel spokes. The figures of a golden lion and unicorn stood on the top like a decoration on top of a cake. By the time I caught the whispers of "The King and Queen!", I'd already figured it out. This was the royal carriage itself.

When the groom opened the carriage door, I half expected Cinderella to step out. I wouldn't have known if she had; the crowd pressed in for a closer look and blocked my view. The other servants were standing on tip-toes to see the King and Queen, so I only just caught a glimpse of a plume hat and fur cloak followed by a tall tower of strawberry red ringlets. These disappeared through the archway, along with the Earl, the Countess, Sophia and the most important servants. I got stuck in the crowd following slowly behind. When I finally made it through the doorway and into the courtyard, I happened to glance to my left. In the arched passage that leads to the Horse Court and stables stood Jack Hornsby watching the crowd go by, and behind him, two shadowy figures. I recognised Frederick and Digby right away, and looked around to make sure no one was watching before I crept over to join them.

"Mistress Katie." Jack took of his cap, but at the same time took a step in front of the doorway so as to block my view of the two boys. "Aren't you er ... joining the others?" I quickly solved the obvious: Jack was standing guard for Digby and Frederick.

"Are the boys swapping places now?" I asked, wanting Jack to know I was in on the secret.

"Swapping? Boys?" He was still keeping up the act.

Frederick's hushed voice came from behind. "Is that Katherine? It's alright. She knows and she can help."

Frederick, now in plain linen breeches and a jerkin, was just looking over what appeared to be another him. "You look every bit the courtier, Digby," he said, patting the *other him* on the shoulder. "Here, don't forget your hat."

"Good grief, you two really could be twins!" I whispered.

"Come closer, Katie." Frederick beckoned. I felt rather pleased to be confided in. At least it was reassuring he didn't still suspect me of devilry anymore.

"Do you think it's believable enough?" he asked.

I cocked my head and took a good, long look at Digby. With his hair and whiskers trimmed neatly and his silk suit, high-heeled shoes and lacy collar, he was transformed. I might have taken him for Frederick without a second glance if I hadn't known any better. "Would fool me," I assured them.

"Good. Then off you go, Digby. My aunt the Queen will want an audience with you. Don't worry. She's not seen me since I grew hair on my chin. She won't notice a thing. The Earl on the other hand ... well, best you stand with your back to him when possible." He braced Digby's stiff shoulders, said "Good luck," then looked to me. "Might I employ you to show Digby to the Portrait

Gallery? The Royal Apartments are just off the end of it, to the left."

"What about you?" I asked.

"Me? I'm off to the hayloft for a peaceful evening with the barn swallows and a good book." He tipped his hat (which was actually Digby's) and stepped into the light of the Horse Court, whistling merrily to himself just as Digby might have done.

Poor Digby didn't say a word on our walk to the Portrait Gallery. I could hear him breathing fast, shallow breaths and felt sorry for him. I knew how he felt. After all, I was an imposter at Otterly Manor as well without the slightest idea of how to behave like a courtier. I recalled Sophia's words to me just as Digby and I stepped onto the staircase landing with the wooden leopard. "If you believe you belong here, everyone else will," I said.

He gulped and gave an uncertain nod. But with each step up the next flight of stairs, he seemed to rally. His shoulders relaxed a little, and he held his head higher. We parted ways at the end of the gallery; he went left to the King and Queen's special apartments. I turned into the right wing towards the family's rooms to wait for Sophia in the red bedchamber. I looked back once over my shoulder just to be sure Digby hadn't fainted. Satisfied, I turned back around and nearly rammed right into the velvety chest of Master Van Hoebeek.

I bit my tongue to keep from screaming. He loomed over me, peering down over his woolly beard.

"You were going somewhere?" he asked.

"To Sophia's room," I breathed. "To dress for the

banquet." I noticed his hand rested on the doorknob that led into Frederick's dressing room.

"Ah. Well, I was … just on my way to the Royal Apartments, but I seem to have taken a wrong turn."

"They're just that way." I pointed, hoping he couldn't hear my heart drumming away.

Master Van Hoebeek bowed his head and passed me by with a whoosh of his cape.

Well, that was weird, I thought. But the strange encounter did not cross my mind again … at least not until after the disastrous events of the banquet.

14

A ROYAL DISASTER

*S*ophia and I stood on the Turkish rug, twirling in turns and admiring one another's gowns. It had taken ages to get dressed, but at last we were ready, she in her dark green silk with her golden hair tumbling down the back, and I in my yellow velvet with my hair slicked back by the pearly headband.

"I do wish we could sit together, dear Katie," she said, taking my hands and squeezing them. The King's reception banquet was to be in the Great Hall; Sophia would sit at the High Table with the nobility, and I would slip in hopefully unnoticed among the courtiers at the long tables.

"But at least we will be able to see each other on the dance floor!" I consoled her just before a servant summoned her to join the other High Table folk who would enter the banquet in procession.

A WHISPERED *"Wow!"* escaped me when I stepped into

the Great Hall. It was just like a fairy land. Candles burned on every table and in every windowsill, and a fire blazed in royal reds and golds in the hearth. The light sparkled off the silver serving wear on the tables and the gems and sequins on the courtiers' clothes. The platters themselves were piled high with the most bizarre dishes, from boars' heads to whole peacocks, feathers and all. Swags of greenery were draped along the yellow walls. A deep breath filled my nostrils with the warming smells of pies and roasts and tingling spices.

But better than the smells was the sound that seemed to be floating down from the ceiling. It took me several minutes of turning on the spot to figure out where the beautiful music came from. Then at last I spotted the musicians seated in a sort of balcony above the Great Hall entrance, hidden by a wooden screen carved with the noble Buckville leopards.

I stayed close to the hearth while the cooks darted between all the elegant lords and ladies milling around with goblets in their hands. My idea had been to scope out the room for Tom Tippery, but I knew it was unlikely he'd be at the banquet; he certainly didn't have the courtly airs of his boss. I spied the tall, black-caped figure of Master Van Hoebeek. He had strayed from the crowds and wondered alone around the dais with his goblet in hand, inspecting the portraits on the wall as if he were at an art gallery. My mind flashed back to the blank canvas. In all the excitement of the Court's visit, I had forgotten to tell Sophia about it! We had been so caught up with Frederick's schemes, I hadn't even thought of it since. I would have to tell her after the banquet and see what she made of it.

But I soon lost interest in Master Van Hoebeek and his strange ways because there was simply too much else to take in. I enjoy people watching any and everywhere, but *this* was more like watching a theatrical performance. Everyone moved and laughed and batted their eyelashes as if it had all been rehearsed. I thought of all the balls in princess movies I'd seen as a kid; the real thing was far more grand, and far more strange.

I spotted Jack leaning against the opposite wall from me, and walked, as elegantly as I could, over to meet him. "I didn't know you were attending the banquet," I said over the roar of voices. "I thought servants had to eat in the tents."

"Well, I'm not exactly attending." He spoke in a lowered voice, his eyes darting around. "More like observing. Master Frederick thought I had best keep an eye on … you know." His head gave a twitch towards the High Table, indicating where Digby would be sitting in just a few minutes. "I'm to report back if anything goes amiss."

Before I could respond, a trumpet sounded and a man in purple velvet who looked more pig than human stepped up on the dais. His deep voice rang out like a belch. "Good Lords and Ladies of the Realm, Their Royal Highnesses, the King and Queen of England."

In unison, the entire room became shorter, the men bowing so low they swept the floor with their hats, the ladies melting into their skirts in low curtseys. I tried as best I could to imitate them, but how they folded their legs under their skirts and petticoats, I will never guess. I hoped nobody would notice when I lifted my head just a little so that I could watch the High Table procession. I recognised King James from the many portraits I'd seen. He entered first in his great fur cloak and sat on a throne in the middle of the table. Queen Anne with her white, powdered face followed and sat beside him. Then the Earl and the Countess took their places, and several other important-looking people including one in bishop's robes, and finally Sophia followed by Digby. Jack let out a breath of relief behind me. So far, the stable boy's disguise had fooled them.

Once the High Table guests were seated, the bishop-looking man stood to ask God's blessings on the King and Queen, the Earl and Countess and on the meal. As soon as that was done, the courtiers took their seats at the long tables. I hesitated, not sure where I should go, but Jack nudged me to the closest open seat, and I slid in as quickly as I could. I felt I'd happily exchange my seat for Jack's place glued against the wall. But thankfully the people sat around me seemed very merry — I do believe they'd been at the wine long before the banquet began — and the ladies smiled sweetly at me without trying to make much conversation.

I picked at the strange savoury dishes, trying not to think too much about what might be in them. Then sweets were served, and at last the moment Sophia and I had been waiting for arrived: the dance!

The King and Queen danced the first dance, opening the floor for everyone else to join in. I caught Sophia's eye just before she leaned over to whisper to Digby who nodded and made a bee-line for me.

"Might I claim your hand, Mistress Katherine?" He sounded so confident, I thought he'd convinced himself he really was a courtier.

"Yes, thank you ... Frederick." I bit my lip to keep from smiling.

After ten seconds on the floor, all my nerves flew away and I was having the time of my life. After horseback riding, I was sure that dancing must be the best thing in the world, especially when Digby lifted me up and twirled me around like I was floating on air. Sophia danced with a very pompous-looking boy, but we managed to catch eyes throughout the dance without his noticing.

We were well and truly out of breath when the Herald, as I had learned was the piggish man's title, returned to the dais and announced, "For the pleasure of their Majesties and this Court, The King's Men, directed by Master William Shakespeare and under the auspices of our noble King, will now present excerpts from Master Shakespeare's newest play, *Macbeth*." A gleeful murmur moved through the crowds as the actors took the floor, and some shouted out, "Master Shakespeare! ... Oh, how delightful! ... I hear this one is ghastly frightful. His greatest work yet!"

I realised with a start that my mouth was hanging open like a codfish's. Was I actually going to see the *real* William Shakespeare? This night really did feel like a Midsummer Night's Dream!

A man with a broad forehead and a fashionably pointed beard walked out across the floor to the applause of all. I recognised him without a doubt. After all, Nan and

Pop took Charlie and me to visit his house in Stratford-upon-Avon many times over the years.

Master Shakespeare thanked the King and Queen for their royal patronage, then introduced the play in rhyme. All the courtiers applauded once again, and the play began.

I had seen Shakespeare's plays at the Globe Theatre in London, but they were nothing to compare with this production. I was so bewitched, I nearly forgot to spare a glance at Sophia to see what she thought of it. She too watched in wonder. Digby gaped as if he were gazing into heaven. The Queen smiled, and even King James whose deep, sunk eyes looked a little vacant or bored before, appeared spellbound.

My skin prickled with goose bumps as the three Weird Sisters — *played by men in hideous makeup* — started their wicked revelry. They whooped and danced wildly around a cauldron, chanting *double, double, toil and trouble* louder and louder and louder. And then ...

An agonised scream echoed off the yellow walls and shook the panes of glass. Every single body in the hall gasped, even the actors. The scream hadn't come from the them but from behind, from the dais.

There was a loud scuffle as chairs scooted back. All at the High Table but the King were out of their seats, gathering around something on the floor. The Bishop pushed through them and knelt down in the middle of their huddle. After a minute of deathly silence, he stood again, looked to the King and solemnly proclaimed out across the crowd, "The Earl of Dorset is dead."

15

MIDSUMMER NIGHT'S MAYHEM

*S*hock rippled through the Great Hall. Some prayed, others wept. I tried to get a view of Sophia. There she was, stood behind the Countess who looked like she was in complete shock. Sophia was holding her hand and stroking it. The King was whispering orders, and men in black gowns rushed in to carry off the body. But before they could even drape a sheet over the Earl, another shout added to the confusion.

"Your Majesty! Your Majesty!" Master Van Hoebeek pushed through the crowds to stand in the middle of the floor, right where we had danced and the Weird Sisters had revelled moments before. Was this still all part of the night's theatrical production? Master Van Hoebeek dragged a young woman in plain, dirty clothes behind him by the arm. Her face was smudged with dirt, but her enormous, terrified eyes shone like harvest moons.

For the first time, the King actually stood up. He held up a hand to silence the hall, then turned his sunken eyes towards Master Van Hoebeek and the woman. "Speak, sir.

What matter is this that brings you before us with such exigency?"

Master Van Hoebeek bowed, still gripping the wild-eyed woman's wrist. "Forgive me, Sire. Nothing but the direst concern for your person's own safety compels me to come before you. The Earl's death was not of natural cause, but of *murder*."

Another gasp rose from the room. The King's face might have been a portrait. It did not change. He merely turned his dead eyes to the Bishop who had examined the Earl's body.

The Bishop shrugged. "Your Majesty, the foamy white substance erupting from his lordship's mouth *does* suggest some dark power at work."

Several women swooned and fainted at the mention of either the foam or the dark power.

The painter pressed on. "And not only murder, but murder of the darkest, most devilish manner. Witchcraft!"

At that word, I'm sure I saw the King's eyes grow larger, and his mouth opened and closed. It was with a much croakier voice that he demanded, "What reason have you to presume this is the work of witches?"

"This woman," — Van Hoebeek swung her around by her wrist so that she let out a little cry of pain — "was caught lurking in the family's quarters. She admits to being practised in the devilish arts."

"Is this true, wench?" the King croaked.

She looked so distraught, and when she didn't answer, Master Van Hoebeek gritted his teeth and shook her by the wrist. She looked at him with terror in her eyes and answered through sobs, "Ay, Your Majesty."

The King's eyes positively bulged. "And do you confess before God and His appointed King to have employed the magical arts to murder the noble Lord Buckville?"

When she only gaped, Master Van Hoebeek spoke for her again. "The woman confessed to me that she did not plot the murder herself, Your Majesty, but acted as a consultant to the true conspirator. It was he who gave her entry into this house and lodged her in his own chambers. And I have reason to believe, Sire, that he would not have stopped at the Earl, but might have caused harm to your own esteemed life."

The King's face went red. "WHO IS THE PERPETRATOR?"

A small, lifeless voice escaped the woman's lips. "The man who consulted with me to curse the Earl takes wine and meat with you, Your Majesty." She spoke as if she were reading lines from a page. She sounded like the worst actor in my sixth-grade school play. "He told me he was the Earl's heir and could not wait any longer for his inheritance. He is that man there." She hung her head and pointed a shaking finger at Digby. "Ll-lord ..." she stuttered.

"Lord ... Frederick?" Master Van Hoebeek growled through gritted teeth.

"Ay. Lord Frederick."

My blood went icy cold. I crumpled down onto the bench as my legs turned to mush. All I could do was watch the terrible drama unfold. Men with helmets and swords charged the dais and bound up Digby's hands. He didn't even try to defend himself. *But where was Sophia?*

And then I saw her, struggling to break free from the Lord Steward and Nurse Joan as they led her away from the dais and out into the antechamber.

I had to do something. I forced myself to stand up on my jelly legs and swung around desperately looking for Jack. I saw him; he was trying to push his way through the crowds to the door.

"Jack!" I screeched. Thankfully he turned and came right for me, bending down to my height and swinging his cape over my shoulder to whisper in my ear, "Tell no one."

Was he serious? "But we have to tell them the truth. Digby doesn't know what to do. They'll kill him!"

Jack looked as serious as a funeral. "If they find out he's not really Frederick, they will surely kill him for deception and conspiracy. The only hope for either of them now is for us to hide Master Frederick until we can find a way to prove his innocence. I must go to him at once. Speak to Mistress Sophia, but remember: *Tell no one*." And he was gone.

16

POWDER, TREASON AND PLOT

*T*he banquet guests dispersed after Digby's arrest. The Countess was whisked away from the hall by a flurry of maids while armed guards escorted the King and Queen. I stood still for a while, letting the world move around me like a stormy sea. Only when several teary kitchen maids began clearing tables did I dare to move.

Should I go to the stables first so I could bring Sophia a report of exactly what had become of the real Frederick? I decided it was too risky; I might give away his hiding place. Better to speak to Jack after things quietened down and then find out where Frederick was hiding. Just then, I thought, Sophia needed a friend more than anything.

Having decided to make my way directly up to the red bedchamber, I crossed the hall, went up the staircase and tip-toed down the Portrait Gallery as always; only when I got to the end of it, where normally I'd turn right to enter the family's quarters, two guardsmen blocked my way with crossed spears.

"Name and purpose," one of them demanded looking right over my head.

"Katherine Watson." I clenched my fists at my sides, hoping the guard wouldn't see my shaking. "I'm Mistress Sophia's companion."

The guard eyed me suspiciously, but thankfully stepped aside to let me pass. The first door on the right to Frederick's chambers was open, and two more guards were inside peeking under carpets and in the hearth as if searching for something, but I couldn't linger in case the guards behind me changed their minds and threw me out for snooping.

It turned out the guards were only the first obstacle, and hardly the most frightening. Sitting outside Sophia's door was the last person I wanted to see: Nurse Joan.

I did my best to sound polite when I asked her, "May I go in?" She scowled at me and looked as though she wasn't going to allow it. Then, to my huge relief, she swiftly stood up to let me to the door.

"What the Mistress needs is a good night's sleep," she snapped. "Not a lot of girlish prattle."

I nodded before turning the door handle and pushing it open a crack. I'd expected to find Sophia in a pool of tears — that's probably where I'd be if my brother had just been accused of conspiring to murder — but instead, she sat on her couch in front of the fire with Tannia's big head in her lap and stared into the flames. Both looked up when I closed the door behind me, and Sophia jumped to her feet and lifted her skirts to rush over and throw her arms around my neck. I hugged her back.

"Katie, I am so glad to see you." We sat together on the

couch. "My head is all confusion. I need your help. I tried to speak to the Countess, to tell her it was all a mistake, but they refused to let me see her and dragged me off here like *I* was their prisoner as well as Frederick!"

"I know," I said, wishing I had anything to say that could help. "But maybe it's best you didn't speak to the Countess." I explained what Jack Hornsby had said, and how he had urged me to say nothing to anybody for both Frederick and Digby's sakes.

Sophia pinched her eyebrows together and bit her lip in deep thought. "Yes, Jack Hornsby is right. The only thing we can do is to prove Frederick's innocence and exonerate him. Then he can come out of hiding, and Digby can return to the stables as if none of it ever happened ... But where do we start?" She looked into my eyes as if hoping to find the answer.

And of course the answer came to me easily. Anyone who knows the least thing about detective stories would have known the first step to solving a mystery. "We need a list of suspects," I said confidently. "If we could just find evidence of who really murdered the Earl, we can make a case to the King."

"Yes!" Sophia looked hopeful for half a second. "That is ... if he will hear us. But who would wish to murder the Earl? He has no enemies that I can think of. He was a godly and respected lord, more interested in scholarly matters than politics. Not unlike Frederick."

I rested my chin in my hand and tried to think. Closing my eyes tightly, I replayed the entire evening, searching my memory for some detail I might've missed. At least that technique always worked for Sherlock

Holmes. "What exactly happened up there, on the dais?" I asked.

"The Earl was choking before he died," Sophia said. "He held his throat and a sort of white foam, like the foam on the top of a pint of ale, bubbled up out of his mouth."

I grimaced. "Sounds more like poison than a curse to me."

"*Genau!* I too do *not* believe he was cursed, nor that Bessy Tippery is really a witch."

"Bessy Tippery?" I asked in disbelief.

"Oh yes, I forgot you've never seen her. That girl who accused Frederick was Tom Tippery's daughter, Bessy. The one who was so kind to me. She can't be a witch! She's a Christian woman if ever I met one, and anyway, I do not believe she has ever even laid eyes on Frederick before."

"Although …" I hesitated, because the thought playing in my mind sounded insane even to me. But then, here I was in the seventeenth century. Anything might be possible. "Are you sure she's not really a … a you know. I mean, after all, Tom brought me here by *some* kind of magic."

Sophia's eyes searched about uncertainly. "Yes, but Katherine, you heard what I said to Frederick. Whatever power Tom used to bring you here, it was not the devil's work. Witches are believed to put hexes on their neighbours, to make their cows' udders dry up or their crops fail. A mere witch could not have performed the magic that brought you here. It was nothing short of … of a miracle!"

I couldn't argue with Sophia's logic. "So then you think somebody put Bessy up to framing Frederick? She *did* sound far too rehearsed to be genuine."

"Yes, I am certain somebody was using her. But who?"

I tried to call up the faces of all the people in the Great Hall that night. Could it have been one of the servants? Or maybe … "Tom Tippery was missing from the banquet," I blurted. "But then why would he put his own daughter in danger? No, that doesn't make sense."

Sophia shook her head. "And besides, Tom was so kind to me, I cannot believe that he could be my guardian's attacker. Or my brother's for that matter. If Tom is involved, he must be following another's instructions."

Something she said flipped a switch in my brain. "You mean like an apprentice?" *Could it be? If Tom had been willing to paint for Master Van Hoebeek and give away all the credit, might he also be willing to kill for him?* I stood up and paced back and forth in front of the fire. The pieces were falling into place now. My strange encounters with Master Van Hoebeek had always left me feeling uneasy, though I couldn't say why. Then there was the blank canvas incident … and tonight, his eagerness to accuse Frederick … There were still many pieces of the puzzle missing, but I just knew it had to be him. "I can't believe I didn't see it before!" I groaned. Stopping in my tracks, I turned to Sophia. "Master Van Hoebeek is no artist. He's a murderer!"

Sophia's eyes were as doubtful as a doe's at first, but they turned as fierce as a tiger's as I told her all about Master Van Hoebeek's deception, using Tom to do his work and cover his tracks for him.

"To think!" she said at last. "I've been sitting right in front of that monster for days. How could I be so blind?" With her hands balled into fists in her lap, she looked ready to fight. "That explains how Master Van Hoebeek appeared so quickly on the scene with Bessy. He must have been rehearsing her lines with her even whilst the King's Players recited theirs. But then, that *is* odd ... " She laid a finger to her cheek.

"What is?" I asked.

"Master Van Hoebeek came in from the antechamber with Bessy only seconds after the horrible scene. If he wasn't even in the room, how do you think he managed to murder the Earl?"

I gnawed my lip thinking. The answer hit me, and I hit my forehead with my open palm. "Duh!" I groaned, then noticed the bewildered look on Sophia's face. "*Duh* means ... oh never mind. I just remembered something. Before you all came into the banquet, Master Van Hoebeek was loping around the dais, *pretending* to look at the paintings. He could easily have slipped poison into the Earl's goblet without anyone noticing!" It all fit, all made sense. If Sophia hadn't been so distraught, I'd have felt quite smug about my detective skills at that moment. Charlie would be proud.

There was a tap at the door, and Tatty and Elinor came in to help us out of our ball gowns. I shivered when the velvet gown came off and the night air pricked my skin. The door creaked open again and Nurse Joan entered, turning the room a little bit colder with her scowl. Had that woman ever smiled in her life? I might as well have tried to picture Master Van Hoebeek in a tutu.

To be fair to Nurse Joan though, no one was smiling tonight.

"Get your sleep, Sophia," she said in what I think was

an attempt at a gentle voice. "On the morrow you shall appear before the King to give an account of your brother's words and deeds since returning to this house."

"And if the King will not listen to the truth?" Sophia asked, her head held high like a queen's.

"It is insolence to question the King's judgement, Mistress. He is God's appointed."

"Yes, but he is not God himself. Elsewise he would not suffer from such a fright of demons and witches!"

Nurse Joan shot a fierce finger to her thin lips to hush her. "Mistress," she hissed. "Do not speak of such things on a night such as this. Have we not been plagued enough by evil, that you would invite the devil's servants to do us more mischief? Even now the stewards are marking the doors and hearths with the witches' marks for the King and Queen's protection."

Sophia crossed her arms. "Tell the stewards I should like no witches' mark placed on *my* hearth. The Earl is dead and my brother is on trial for murder. *I* prefer to pray for protection." She spun around, marched to the bedside, knelt down. Her lips moved, though the words were silent."

Realising it was useless to scold Sophia any further, Nurse Joan looked at me as if I'd just insulted her. I was grateful when she picked up her skirt and strode out of the room with Tatty and Elinor following meekly behind.

WE DID PRAY THAT NIGHT, silently side-by-side. And as I prayed for Digby and Frederick, I imagined how I would feel in Sophia's place with my world upside down and my own brother in grave danger. This was not the adventure I'd imagined or hoped for. But maybe … just maybe … this was the reason I had been brought back in time, to be a friend to Sophia when she needed one most. Maybe she was right. I was here by a miracle. And if a miracle is what I'd been given, I decided there on my knees, I *would* make the most of it.

But as I drifted off to sleep, another sickening thought crept in to eat away at my resolve, like a storm cloud snuffing out the sun. If Tom Tippery *was* somehow tied up in the Earl's murder, it was possible, even likely, that he had fled the scene, and with him my way of getting home. My best hope was if he had stayed to be near his daughter, but then his mind would be preoccupied with graver matters than helping some little girl get back home again.

What if I was stuck in this world of petticoats and frilly lace forever? In that moment, I felt I'd give up all the adventures in the world just to see my family again. It was all I could do to squeeze my eyes shut and pray it wasn't too late.

THE BLACK SHEEP

*T*he next morning, I didn't say a word to Sophia of the worrying questions crowding my mind. She was to go straight after breakfast into the King's hearing, and I could tell she was anxious. I would have to wait and wonder the morning away on my own and pray for the best, meanwhile trying not to think about Tom Tippery or let the hundred *what-ifs* in the back of my brain get the better of me.

Over breakfast, I tried to focus on helping Sophia prepare for the frightening task of speaking with the King. "Do you think you'll be able to speak privately with the King, so you can say it was Master Van Hoebeek without him listening in and denying it?"

She shook her head. "It is not likely. But I shall not let Master Van Hoebeek intimidate me. I shall not even look in his direction when I speak to the King." Violently ripping her bread roll in half, she added, "Truth *will* prevail." Neither of us had much appetite for breakfast, but at least it was something to do while we waited for

Sophia's summons ... and the bread was proving a good outlet for Sophia's anger.

"If only we knew *why* Master Van Hoebeek wanted the Earl dead," I said for the tenth time, attacking my boiled egg with my knife.

"Yes, if only." Sophia sighed. "I have thought and thought and can think of no reason he should wish to kill his patron."

"Still," — I tried to sound hopeful — "he is so obviously guilty. The King would have to be an idiot not to see it."

A rap at the door made us both start. Nurse Joan had come for Sophia.

"Will the Countess be present?" Sophia asked, doing her best to sound confident.

Nurse Joan sniffed. "My Lady the Countess is unwell and keeps to her bedchamber."

Sophia closed her eyes, took a deep breath and let it out again. When she opened her eyes, we both smiled weakly, each trying to reassure the other. She stood, dusted off her skirts, and followed Nurse Joan into the corridor. The door closed, and the torturous wait began.

I tried to sit still by the fire and read *The Hound of the Baskervilles*, but every little creak of a floorboard or crack of the fire made me look up and lose my place. Not to mention the drama of Sherlock Holmes had become somewhat overshadowed by my own, real life ordeal.

I had finally given up reading and was lying curled up on the velvet sofa with my eyes closed when the door creaked open. It was Sophia at last. I bolted upright, dying for the news, but I could see straight away from her flushed cheeks that things had not gone as we'd hoped.

The words came out so flat they might have been an automated recording. "Master Van Hoebeek is gone."

"Gone? But where ... how did he leave without the King's guards knowing?"

"The King gave him leave to go. Apparently the *master*" — she said the word with mocking disdain — "had an important commission from the Dutch Court and could not be detained another day."

"But then it's obvious, isn't it? He's hit the road before anyone could find evidence that he's the murderer. Did you tell the King about the blank canvas?"

Sophia plopped down on the couch beside me and stared into the fire. I was startled to see her usually keen and sparkling eyes so empty of hope. "I tried to tell him, but he gave me no ear. His verdict was made before I even spoke. His own obsessive fear that witches are plotting his ruin has blinded him to any other possibility than that Frederick is guilty of conspiring with one."

I couldn't believe my ears. My blood was boiling with the injustice of it all. "But what evidence is there other than the testimonies of a fake painter and a frightened girl?"

"That is the worst part." Sophia's face was still as stone, but for the first time since all this had begun, a tear tumbled down her cheek to fall into her open hand. "The guards have found a witch's herb bag and curse-summoning marks on the floor in Frederick's dressing chamber."

Both my hands flew up to cover my gaping mouth.

"But how ... ?" Then I remembered. "Oh wait ... " I snapped my fingers as another piece clicked in place. "I know how! Just before the banquet, just after Digby joined you in the Royal Apartments, I had another run in with Master Van Hoebeek, and he was just outside Frederick's room. He planted that evidence while everyone else was busy getting ready for the banquet!"

Another tear followed the first into Sophia's hand. "Oh Katie, it all makes so much sense! But what good will it do? The King has determined to send Frederick, or Digby rather, to be tried as a nobleman at the Tower of London. And poor Bessy will hang right here at the Manor unless her confession can save her. So you see, she's bound to confess the very lie Master Van Hoebeek made her proclaim to all the Court. Telling the truth now might cost her her life."

I couldn't deny that this was a true predicament. What would the testimony of two little girls count for if everyone else confirmed that Frederick was guilty ... unless we could persuade others of the truth. "Isn't there anyone here who will listen to you? What about the Queen? She's your aunt, right? Won't she speak to the King for you?"

Sophia stroked Tannia's head as if she were trying to rub off some luck. "Queen Anne did not attend the hearings. I think ..." She swallowed, and continued in a hollow voice. "A queen must choose her connections very carefully. If my family should become disgraced in this matter, she would not wish to remind anyone of our connection."

"But that's terrible!" I protested. "Well then who else will listen? The Countess?"

Another tear fell as she shook her head. "Nurse Joan says the Countess is indisposed ever since watching her husband die in front of her. No one can see her. However," — she laid a finger to her cheek, thinking — "there *is* someone who could speak for us. The Earl's younger brother, Baron Buckville, has sent word. He arrives today to see to the Earl's affairs. As the Earl's ward and heir, Frederick should be the one, of course. But now it falls to the next in line."

"The Baron. Oh, you mean Mr Fancy Pants!"

Sophia gave me a pondering look.

"I mean, yes. I've seen the Baron's portrait. Well that's something. Surely the Earl's own brother will help us, won't he?"

"I am not so certain. Lord Buckville and the Baron were not on good terms. I do not know the particulars; the Earl and Countess rarely spoke of him. But when they did, they used their own name for him."

"What was that?" I asked, puzzled.

"Baron Black Sheep."

"Black Sheep? Why?"

"I suppose because his family are ashamed of him. He is a hard, greedy sort of man, I think. There is tale that he drove his first wife to the grave so that he could sell her lands for profit. I know for certain that he fell out of favour with Queen Elizabeth and felt cheated when she bestowed this house on his brother."

"Why is he coming here then? If he and the Earl never spoke, it seems strange that he would be the one to settle the Earl's affairs."

"Yes, but with Frederick in prison, the Baron is the

closest kinsman. It may be he means to marry the Countess. She is wealthy and respected by all the Court. She would restore him to the Crown's good graces. It is a good match for him."

"But for her?" I asked.

Sophia huffed. "I would have to be out of my wits to marry a man my own husband loathed. But for all we know, she *may* be out of her wits." Sophia's shoulders drooped. She looked so tired. It was one of those rare moments when I remembered that under the gowns and elegant manners, she was just a girl my own age, though an extraordinarily brave girl. Seeing my friend look so helpless, my resolve to help her in her hour of need burbled up again.

"Well then there's hope, isn't there? Even if the Baron is hard and greedy, if he wants to impress the Countess, then surely he'll help her ward! We've got to try. When does he come?"

Another knock at the door made us both look up. It was Tatty. She curtseyed before giving her announcement. "Baron Buckville has just arrived, Mistress. Says he wishes to speak to you and offer you his service."

"Thank you, Tatty," Sophia said, wiping her eyes with her handkerchief and straightening up to sit tall once again. "Tell him I'll come as soon as I am composed."

"But Mistress," Tatty whispered. "He's here. In the corridor." She gestured wildly with her head as if to make sure we got the message.

"He is?" Sophia sounded taken aback. She stood and shook out her skirts, and I followed her example. "Very well, Tatty. I am ready for him."

But I don't think either of us was truly ready for the Baron. A slow and heavy clacking of heels against the corridor floorboards announced his coming and, for what reason I don't know, made me hug my stomach to stop it fluttering. Tatty bowed low as the tower of a man stepped over the threshold. I followed Sophia's lead and curtseyed, catching a glimpse of the pom-pom shoes I'd laughed at in the Baron's portrait.

But I did not dare so much as snigger in the presence of the *real* Baron. He seemed to fill the room from the moment he entered it. Sure, his clothes were still ridiculously frilly. But now, in person, he looked more like a proud panther than a poodle.

The Baron surveyed the room with a look of disinterest before his pitch dark eyes ever landed on us. He did not say anything at first, but merely stroked his pointed goatee and examined us down his long, hawk-like nose. After an uncomfortable few seconds, the ends of his moustache curled up and he tilted his head in a bow, extending one silk-stockinged leg at the same time. "Mistress Sophia, it is my privilege to present myself to you, Baron Roger Buckville of Chudleigh, your late guardian's brother." His voice was deep but cold. "How regrettable we should meet under such … *tragic* circumstances." He paused for a short moment, then continued. "As your elder brother is most inopportunely confined and awaiting trial, I have taken upon myself the oversight of Otterly Manor …"

"And the Countess?" Sophia broke in.

"Ah." His face turned seamlessly tragic. "I fear the Countess is most unwell. I have offered her my assistance here, and she has most gratefully accepted it."

Sophia shot me a sideways glance. So her suspicions were true. The Baron *did* mean to marry the Countess. She turned back and made a little curtsey. "We thank you for your service during this trying time, sir."

"Yes." The Baron smiled coldly before wandering over to the window, clacking with each step and stroking his beard. "My lady, in light of last night's distressing events, the Countess is fearful for your safety." He reached the middle of the room and spun around. "I promised her I would keep a close watch over you. And so, in honour of my promise, you shall henceforth be attended by maids from my own household, well-bred girls whom I know that I can trust." His eyes wandered over to me as he pronounced the word *trust*. "Also, you will attend the King's audience with me. After all," — he stepped closer — "you are nearly of an age to attend Court yourself. I shall await you in the gallery while you prepare yourself."

Sophia was as composed as a statue, but I could tell the Baron gave her the creeps as much as he did me. "And what of Katherine? My lady in waiting will, of course, attend with me?"

"Sophia," — the Baron raised an arrogant eyebrow — "it is time you prepared yourself to be a lady at Court and gave up your childhood companions." This time he looked at me directly and smiled his frosty smile. "Surely my own ladies will be company enough for you."

"Thank you, but I will not sleep if Katherine is not beside me. I will surely be woken by night terrors remembering the poor Earl's death."

The Baron's smile had become more of a grimace by now. It dawned on me that, under all the polite chit-chat, he and Sophia were locked in a battle of wills, and I was in the middle of the cross-fire. Sophia had understood the high stakes before I did. If she lost, the Baron would separate us.

He was losing his patience. With sharpness, he replied, "One of my ladies will be your bed companion from now on. They are of worthy breeding as befits a lady of your rank."

Sophia's chin rose a bit higher. She reached out to clasp my hand. "I'd rather have Katherine, thank you."

The Baron did not even pretend to smile anymore. He ground his teeth together, making his pointy, bearded chin wiggle in agitation. "Mistress Sophia, I may have failed to mention that I have certain ... connections that might persuade the King to offer your brother exile rather than execution. Frederick may even be able to return to Germany." He took a step closer so that he was peering down his nose at Sophia. "But all that depends entirely on your cooperation."

Like a warrior, Sophia held his gaze. "What *connections* do you have? I thought you were out of favour at Court."

His yellow teeth flashed in a snarl, but he composed himself, tugging at his lacy collar. "Let me make myself quite clear, mademoiselle. Do as I bid you. Your brother's life depends upon it."

I could feel Sophia's heart beating through her hand. She stood frozen in a staring contest with the Baron for several seconds; then, defeated, she let out a heavy breath and my hand dropped to my side.

"Good girl." The Baron's cold smile returned. He held out his arm and waited for her to take it. Only when they'd reached the door did she look over her shoulder with the sorrow-filled eyes I had first seen in her portrait. Tannia padded dutifully across the floor to Sophia's heel. The door closed behind her, the Baron's heels clacked away down the corridor, and I was alone.

18

NEW DUTIES

$\mathcal{N}$obody ever tells you about the water maid in history class. It's all kings and politicians, scientists and artists, and sometimes playwrights. But if ever I were to become a history teacher, I would devote a whole class, maybe even a whole chapter to the water maid. I don't think anybody in the history of England worked harder. And I should know. I've been one.

Not a quarter of an hour after the Baron swept Sophia away, just when I thought it could get no worse, the last person I wanted to see in the world appeared at the door: Nurse Joan.

"The Baron has appointed new ladies in waiting to the Mistress," she said, looking as close to happy as I'd seen her. "I am to show you to your new quarters and then instruct you in your new duties." I didn't like the sound of that. I had never doubted for a minute that Nurse Joan, for whatever superstitious reasons of her own, wanted me out of Otterly Manor. If only she'd known at that moment how much I wanted out of it too, to get out of this dreadful predicament and back into my own life. But of course I didn't tell her that. I didn't say a word. I collected up my few things from around the room — my book, notebook and Oscar's sling and tennis ball — stuffed them all into my backpack and readied myself to follow her to my new quarters.

Nurse Joan eyed my backpack as if I kept a baby python inside of it. I suppose she thought my belongings as strange and threatening as she thought I was, with my devil-kissed hair; but I hardly bothered just then what she thought. I held my chin up high, the way Sophia did when she faced challenges. *How could even you make the most of this situation, Sophia?* How I wished I could ask her.

I nearly had to run to keep up with Nurse Joan's soldier-like march as she led me along the Portrait Gallery. At the end of it, instead of turning right to take the Great Staircase, she turned left to face the panelled wall, laid her hands against one of the panels, and pushed. It gave a creak and opened. Just like the secret door the Green Man guarded, the hinges were invisible so that you'd never detect a door hidden in the woodwork. Behind the panel was a steep, winding staircase lit by candles on little ledges.

Nurse Joan stopped at the top of the stairs. With the candlelight gleaming in her hawk eyes, she looked as menacing as an old hag. "You will use the servant's stairs from now on," she said, then lifted her skirt and started down — *clop, clop, clop* — step after step until at last we reached the dark, cold bottom which led into a narrow corridor. It amazed me to think that I'd not even seen half of this enormous hive of a house. Normally on a tour of an old house, I find the servants' quarters interesting; but I had a horrible sinking feeling about them now, with Nurse Joan as my guide.

No decorations had been wasted on this hidden part of the house. Plain walls and stone floors were good enough for the workers. The right wall of the corridor was lined with plain, wooden doors, evenly spaced. Nurse Joan stopped in front of one of the doors, turned a squeaky wooden doorknob, and pushed it open. The small, grey room was dark and cold. The only light came from a narrow window too high up to see out of. There was no furniture, only three straw beds tucked into the room's cobwebby corners.

"Tatty sleeps here and Elinor there." She made sharp gestures with her head towards two of the straw beds, then turned toward the corner with the third bed. "That one is yours."

My throat tightened up with a hard lump growing in it; but I tried with all my might not to let my face give away what I was feeling. Compared to the red bedchamber with its ever-crackling fire, latticed windows with views of the park, and downy-soft bed, this room felt like a chicken coop.

"Well don't just stand there gawking!" Nurse Joan barked. "Put away your things and change your clothes. The work won't wait!" She shoved a bundle of fabric into my chest and slammed the door.

Thankfully she waited outside while I changed. I needed the privacy to take a few deep breaths to hold back the tears that were forcing their way up to freedom. I took off my fine, blue dress and pulled on a scratchy pair of woollen tights and a brown linen frock. Thankfully it buttoned up the front, and I was able to get it on myself without asking Nurse Joan for help. Finally I tied on my apron and snuggled my precious few belongings down into the straw mattress. *I will make the most of this. I will.* I promised silently as if Sophia could hear me, or maybe it was my mum I spoke to. How I wished *she* were there instead of the prickly old woman tapping her foot impatiently outside the door.

Only when we reached the end of the corridor and came into the kitchens did I understand where in the house we were. One side of the kitchens led into the Buttery which was just off the Great Hall. The other end opened out into kitchen gardens, the brewery and — I suddenly remembered from the plaque in the window — the manor's jail! Which meant I was within yards of Digby and Bessy's cells. But the working part of the house crawled with servants like an ant farm. I'd never be able to try to speak to them without someone seeing me.

"Listen well, girl. You'll take your orders from Mary Hayes, Head Kitchen Matron."

A round woman with a few extra chins bustled over from the big blob of dough she'd been kneading. She looked me over as she wiped her fat, floury hands on her apron, nodding a bit frantically. "She'll do, maam."

"You are answerable to Mary," Nurse Joan continued, clearly enjoying every moment of putting me in my place now that Sophia was not there to stand up to her. "Shirk your duties and Mary will report to me, and *I* will report directly to the Baron. Am I understood?"

I nodded, afraid that my voice would crack if I spoke.

"Good," was all she said before swooshing past me. I would have breathed a sigh of relief to hear her clopping footsteps retreat down the corridor, but Mary Hayes didn't give me the chance.

She was a woman of few words, although when she *did* speak, she bellowed and commanded immediate action. "Water," she boomed, then waddled over to where a wooden beam with two buckets attached to ropes on either end was leaning against the kitchen wall. "Put this on." She lifted the thing like it weighed the same as a toothpick; but when she set it down on my shoulders, I nearly toppled over from the unexpected weight. "Fill both pails in the river. Bottom of the hill, near the mill. Make haste!"

I didn't have a clue how to get to the river, or that the Manor even *had* a mill. But Mary Hayes didn't seem in a mood for questions, so I wobbled away, turning sideways to fit through the door. Once in the kitchen gardens, I shifted the beam on my shoulders so that I could get my balance. I had to ask three servants for directions before feeling confident I could find the mill. The first was a gardener who just said, "Bottom of the hill," and carried on cutting his lettuces. I knew of only one hill, the one Pop had driven up that day that seemed an age away; so I headed around to the front of the house, taking stock as I passed of the two royal guards outside the jail.

When I got to the front of the house, I realised the ground sloped away in every direction. The river could be any which way, and I wasn't about to trudge down the wrong hill with that ox yoke on my shoulders. I asked a servant threshing hay, who at least pointed in a particular direction. Many heavy steps later, I asked another servant grazing pigs under the trees who told me I was not half an hour from the mill, which made me want to throw off the yoke, sit down and wallow with the pigs.

I had no idea Otterly Park was so massive! It must have covered half the county of Kent! About half an hour later, after winding through tall bracken and dense forest, I finally spotted something at the bottom of the hill which I thought must be the mill at last. But when I got closer, I saw it was just the wheel of an old abandoned wagon all overgrown with ivy vines. I sat down on a rock to wipe the sweat out of my eyes before carrying on. Quite soon after, I *finally* came to the river and followed it to the mill where men were hauling stalks of wheat and big burlap sacks. I found a little path down the bank and dipped my buckets into the current, one then the other. When I stood again, my legs shook beneath me.

I'm quite strong from years of riding, but the walk up that hill under the weight of all that water, trying desperately to keep it from sloshing out, was without a doubt the hardest work I have ever done. When I had climbed high enough to see Otterly Manor's battlements above the tree line, I was so relieved that I didn't notice the wagon rut in the mud. I tripped, throwing out my hands to brace my fall. Before I could stop it, the beam slipped off my shoulder and both buckets turned on their sides. I just sat in the newly-made mud, huffing and puffing and sniffling for several minutes. But at the end of them, there was only one thing to do. *Back down the hill.*

At last, I triumphantly laid those two buckets of water at Mary Hayes's feet, only to receive a disapproving look.

"What took you so long?" She grabbed the buckets from me, and I didn't know whether to laugh or cry when she emptied them into a big stone bowl and said, "Another two trips should do it."

BY THE TIME I crawled onto my straw mattress that night, I was too tired even to mind its scratchiness or to miss the goose down pillow I'd grown used to. In fact, I was too tired to think about or feel anything at all except for my aching shoulders, back and legs. I was glad Tatty and Elinor were already asleep on their own mats; they wouldn't hear me groan as I tried — *and failed* — to get comfortable so I could fall into wonderful oblivion. Despite the cramps all over my body, sleep pulled me under in no time. I dreamt I was doggy paddling in a giant bucket of water. Someone was knocking from the outside, someone trying to get in to rescue me. I kept paddling. The someone kept knocking, a little harder, a little harder ...

I opened my eyes. The knock came again, on the bedroom door. Tatty was up with a shawl around her shoulders. She opened the door just a crack, letting a beam of quivering candle light spill in. A man's hushed voice spoke, "Is one Katherine Watson within?"

Tatty squinted into the darkness, unsure whether I was or wasn't; but by that time I had hopped up onto my aching legs and shuffled across the straw-covered floor. "I'm Katherine Watson."

The young porter lowered his voice so as Tatty wouldn't overhear. "I'm ordered to deliver this urgent message into your hand."

I took the sealed paper and flipped it over. "Who is it from?"

He licked his lips, his eyes darting up and down the dark corridor. "The sender bids you read the message without delay. I believe her ... or *his* name, as it may be, is enclosed within."

I felt a little silly for asking him who the message was from as it was obviously secret. Sherlock Holmes would never make such a blunder. "Thank you. I shall read it at once," I told him, trying to sound more professional.

I took the note back to bed and waited to hear Tatty's breathing turn slow and even again before opening it. Holding it in the pale puddle of moonlight from the high window, I read:

Katie,

How I hope and pray you are well. The Baron has his eye on me nearly every second, and when he does not, his ladies do. Tomorrow is the King's hunt. The Baron will join him. I will be expected to stand with the other ladies at the front of the house to bid them luck, then I shall try to slip away unnoticed. If you are able, wait for me in the hayloft at 8 o'clock.

My thoughts and prayers are with you!

Your Friend,

Sophia

I folded up the letter and clasped it in my hands all the night long as if holding on to lost hope.

19

WHO DUNNIT

*L*ong before the summer sun woke the next morning, I was awakened by a gentle hand shaking my shoulder. My eyes opened and focused on Elinor kneeling over me.

"Best be getting dressed and to the kitchens, miss."

"Thank you, Elinor." I wearily pushed myself up to my elbow, wincing at the pain in my shoulders. Only then did I remember. *The note!* I sat upright, feeling frantically around my mattress for it. My hand brushed against it under my woollen blanket and I let out a breath of relief. It wasn't that I didn't trust Tatty and Elinor, but one mention of that note to Nurse Joan and the Baron might decide to relocate me to the pigsty next.

I stuck the parchment in between the pages of *The Hound of the Baskervilles* and tucked the book down into my apron. That note would be my lucky charm, reminding me to endure the next three hours knowing that I'd be able to speak to Sophia at the end of them. What we'd be able to come up with to help fix the seemingly hopeless situation remained a looming question. But at least we'd be able to think with our heads together, and that was better than going it alone.

THE KITCHEN STAFF had breakfast in the Great Hall *very* early, before the rest of the household servants. I slid into one of the long tables and ladled some gloopy white stuff into my bowl. The others were sopping it up with chunks of yesterday's bread. When I tried to do the same, I found the bread was rock hard; my jaw ached after the first bite. But I had to eat it. Otherwise I'd fall over dead on my trudge up the hill with the water pails and never see Sophia. That would be simply too tragic. So I took another bite and, as I chewed it to death, looked around the room for some distraction.

Memories of the banquet played out in front of me: Digby's flushed face as he twirled me around the dance floor, laughing with Sophia when the jester grabbed one of the servers and whirled her around. But all that was overshadowed by bitterness now. The Weird Sisters' chant, the horrible scream, the King's blank eyes, Master Van Hoebeek ... I stared at the dais, remembering the whole, horrible drama.

To my horror, my eyes met the dark, swarthy gaze of the Baron's portrait. Why did that stupid painting have to follow me everywhere? There it hung in the centre of the wall behind the High Table, right where the Earl's had been, in the place of honour. The Baron must have taken offence when he found his portrait hanging in a corner and had it moved to the Great Hall. *Master Van Hoebeek sure would be pleased*, I thought with a twist in my stomach. It was just like he had said it would be. That was odd, actually. How could he have known?

That one question sparked my bleary mind into action. Could it be that Master Van Hoebeek had planned for the Baron to take over Otterly Manor the whole time? Could that be the reason he murdered the Earl? Sophia *had* said that after Frederick, the Baron was next in line to inherit Otterly Manor ... which meant that by framing Frederick as the murderer, Master Van Hoebeek had cunningly paved the way for the Baron to steal Frederick's place. *That* would explained the phoney painter's mysterious comments about returning the Baron's portrait to it's *rightful* place ... It would also mean that the Baron was the *true* mastermind behind the Earl's murder. Master Van Hoebeek might only have played the part of hitman.

It all made perfect sense, except for one lingering question: what did Master Van Hoebeek gain in return for doing the Baron's dirty work? As I stewed over my newest theory, it struck me just how similar it all was to *The Hound of the Baskervilles*: the greedy relative willing to murder his own family to get at their inheritance while blaming the murders on superstitious beliefs. Except that in the book, Roger Baskerville committed the murders himself, dressed in a disguise. Only when Sherlock Holmes sees Roger Baskerville's portrait does he make the connection between him and the murderer.

A funny feeling swept over me like a wave. Unaware of all the eyes watching me, I stood up and walked the full length of the Great Hall in a sort of daze. I'm sure the other kitchen staff thought I'd lost it. I didn't stop at the dais, but stepped up and walked around the table, my eyes glued all the while on the Baron's portrait. I stared right into those coal dark eyes as if challenging the Baron to a glaring contest. Then I squeezed my eyes shut and tried to paint a mental picture of Master Van Hoebeek. I wanted to remember *his* eyes, but all I could see in my mind was that great, black woolly beard that looked like sheep's wool. My eyes opened and I mouthed the words that sprung to my mind like a magic spell: *Black Sheep*.

I couldn't believe what I was looking at. It had been a disguise all along, and not even a very good one! How had I not seen it? No one had a real beard like that! It didn't even match the straight, brown wig he'd worn under his hat. But now I could picture the whole face. The long, hawk nose. The dark, hungry eyes when he'd been looking at the Baron's, or rather his own portrait. Master Van Hoebeek was not just a hitman. He was the Baron himself. And now he had control of Otterly Manor.

I reached out my hand to grab the nearest chair back. The room had started spinning with the shock of my discovery. I felt seasick. And at that very moment, a bell rang out, Mary Hayes calling all hands to the kitchen. I walked in a sort of stupor, my heart thudding in my head. How badly I wanted to tell someone, *anyone*, the truth I had just uncovered and expose the Baron for the murderer he truly was! Here they all were, hundreds of servants working around the clock to serve the man who had just murdered their master and would soon murder his heir. But I knew I couldn't say a word, not yet. It would take every drop of my willpower to wait for eight o'clock when I could finally tell Sophia.

20

THE HUNT

I carried my pails of water with extra *umph* that morning, hardly minding the ache in my shoulders. All that mattered was that I got back before the hunt set out, before eight o'clock. The clock on top of the gatehouse tower chimed a quarter to eight just as I neared the house. I hurried to the kitchen to give Mary Hayes my pails, expecting her to send me back out for the second trip as she had done the day before. My heart sank when, after emptying my pails into the big stone bowl, she propped the yoke against the wall. "That'll do for now. You'll help Anna knead the pastry. The Baron will want his game roasted up into pies the minute he's back from the hunt."

Panic blinded me. But I knew if I argued, Mary would turn right around and report me to Nurse Joan, and then I'd really be in pickle. They'd probably put me in the stocks or something. So I gulped, nodded and drifted over to the large table where a wispy maid was pounding a lump of dough with her fist.

"Are you well, love?" she asked when she noticed me standing there like a ghost beside her. "You're pale as a spectre!"

"I'm not feeling so well, actually," I said, my mind firing up again. "I think it may be a fever."

Anna's eyes got big and she took a step backward. "Not the pox, I hope. Lord save us! Why don't you go out to the garden to catch a breath of fresh air? You can pick some sprigs of rosemary and sage from the herb patch while you're about it."

"But Mary Hayes said—"

"Never mind that." Anna shooed me with her floury hand. "Barty will help me with the pastry. Go on."

The relief I felt made me almost dizzy. I couldn't believe the old "get-out-of-school-sick" trick had worked its charm! I could've thrown my arms around Anna, but considering she feared I was pox-infested, I made a bee-line for the door instead while Mary Hayes had her back turned.

The garden was fairly quiet this morning as many of the servants were sending off the hunt. I glanced around to be sure no one watched me, then ran for it as fast as my aching legs would move.

The stables bustled with grooms polishing spurs or saddling up the fastest stallions for the hunters. But most of the noise came from the hitching post where five or six men darted around a huge black horse with ropes and whips. It was Vagabond, and he was most definitely in what my mother would have called a "contrary mood". He reared up and gave a wild whinny, then crashed down stamping his hooves as if he meant to crush the grooms to smithereens just like his unfortunate pigeon victims. One man tried to throw a saddle on the furious horse's back while another two held ropes attached to either side of his bridle which they pulled hard, trying to keep him still. But each time the man with the saddle got close enough to attempt to toss it over Vagabond's back, the horse reared again, throwing the whole lot into confusion.

"That horse has a demon. I told the Earl as much when he took him off my guard. But he was determined to try and break him." My heart jumped into my throat. It was King James who spoke, and standing beside him between the stalls just a stone's throw in front of me was the Baron! I had been so distracted watching Vagabond's protest, I hadn't even noticed them standing there in their hunting coats and boots with muskets slung over their shoulders.

"My late brother thought himself, as with most things, a superior horseman," the Baron answered, then shouted out to the grooms, "Put the animal away. I shall have him exterminated on the morrow to make way for a tame beast."

I had to bite my tongue to keep from erupting with the "No!" that welled up in my chest. The next second, I jumped behind a pile of straw when a melodious woman's voice with an accent that was not *quite* English rang out from behind, causing the King and the Baron to turn around and look at the very spot I had stood watching the only seconds before.

"Are you still not ready, my lords? The entire household has assembled to see us off. The dogs are howling with eagerness. If we do not make haste, every deer in the park will have taken cover 'ere we set out!" It was the Queen, already in the saddle of a beautiful chestnut mare. Through bits of straw, I could see the red plume on her tall hat and the skirt of her dark green riding dress draped over her horse's side.

"You are right, as always, my love," the King answered. "Baron, would you care to select another horse? One perchance with a less murderous temper?"

The Baron responded with a smarmy laugh. The grooms wrestled Vagabond back to his stall while other grooms led out a horse saddled with red and gold tassels, obviously meant for the King. Meanwhile, the Baron ordered another horse for himself. Once the new horse was brought, the two men mounted and trotted out to meet the Queen. I heard the shouts of "Huzzah!" and dogs barking which signalled they'd cantered to the front of the house for their sendoff. This would be the moment for Sophia to slip away unnoticed.

I needed to get to the hayloft quickly, but there was something I had to do first. I knew if I got caught, it would jeopardise everything, but I couldn't ignore what I'd just overheard. I had to rescue Vagabond if I could, though I didn't have a clue how I was going to do it.

Checking the coast was clear, I jumped up from my hiding spot and scampered with my head down past the row of horses' stalls, right to the very last one. Crouched down beside the stall door, I could hear Vagabond's agitated snorts. Suddenly he kicked the door so hard it knocked against the side of my head. I saw stars and the old feeling of panic started to take hold. *No. Not this time.* With clenched fists and gritted teeth, I pushed against the weight of panic and stood up, eye to eye with Vagabond. We stared at each other, both breathing hard. "I'm going to help you," I said, as if I had a plan. I could just see in his eye that he understood I was on his side. Before I knew what was happening, he lowered his enormous head and brushed his nose against my hair. I couldn't move, not until I heard a whisper from behind. "Katie! Mistress Katie!"

I swung around to see Jack Hornsby shouldering a load of hay. He dumped it at his feet and gestured for me to come closer. "What are you doing in here? 'T'ain't safe."

"I'm supposed to be meeting Sophia in the hayloft," I explained.

Jack looked confused by that, then looked down at the clothes I was wearing. "What's the situation in the house? I see you've been made a kitchen wench."

"It's not good, Jack. Sophia has become the Baron's prisoner. I'm never allowed to see her, but she's going to try and meet me while all the fuss is going on around the hunt."

"Good. I'll do my best to keep any prying ears away from the hayloft, then. I want you to give your mistress a message: Frederick is safe."

"Where?" I asked eagerly.

Jack glanced around. "I mustn't tell. Not even you, as it would only compromise your safety. But I will say this. He's been hidden not so far away, and in the last place anyone would think to look for him. But he is sorely tempted to give himself up to rescue Digby from hanging in his place." He glanced around again. "If Mistress Sophia could send a word to persuade him not to do so foolish a thing, I'd be that grateful."

"Coming or not, Jack? King's sounding the horn," one of the groom's shouted, making me duck down.

"I must go," Jack said. "You *will* speak to Mistress Sophia, won't you?"

I promised I would. Jack nodded his thanks, and hurried off before I could say a word.

"Jack, wait!" I whisper-shouted after him. I smiled with relief when his tawny head turned to look over his shoulder, his eyebrows raised in a question. "Sorry. It's just … Vagabond. We have to help him, or the Baron's going to … you know. Can't you do something?"

He drew in a breath through his clenched teeth and squinted in thought. "I'll about try, Mistress. Now you best get on up to that loft before you're seen." And with a nod, he vanished.

THE HAYLOFT PROVIDED the perfect view of the hunting party. From the open door from where the hay was pitched down to the stalls, I watched the Queen waving a handkerchief at the crowds. The Baron sat tall and as proud as a peacock beside her. The King raised his horn and blew. Off the dogs bolted with ear-splitting yelps while the hunters kicked the horses and galloped after them. At the front of the crowd, finely dressed ladies waved handkerchiefs and giggled together. There was no sign of the Countess, but there was a girl with a shawl over her head threading her way through the crowd of servants, away from the giggling ladies in waiting. She was heading for the stables with a great grey dog on her heels. It was Sophia!

A minute later I heard her footsteps on the ladder and ran to the door to give her a hand up. We laughed with relief and hugged each other.

"Oh Katie!" she plopped down on a hay bale to catch her breath. "Thank heavens we made it without getting caught! Though I fear our time may be cut short at any minute."

"I have so much to tell you!" I said. Now I could finally speak to someone, I couldn't hold it back another second, and I blurted, "The Baron murdered Lord Buckville."

Sophia's eyebrows knitted together. "But the Baron wasn't here until after the Banquet ..."

"But Master Van Hoebeek *was*." How I wanted her to see it as clearly as I did.

"You mean to say you believe the Baron hired Master Van Hoebeek to kill the Earl?"

"No. I believe the Baron *is* Master Van Hoebeek. He killed the Earl himself." And I dived right into my explanation: the conversation I'd had with Master Van Hoebeek over the Baron's painting, the sudden appearance of the portrait in place of the Earl's, just as Van Hoebeek had predicted, the sheep's wool beard which was now so obviously a fake.

Sophia's cheeks became more and more flushed with anger as I spoke. When I'd finished, she snapped, "To think that stupid disguise pulled the wool over all our eyes! Master Van Hoebeek always gave me such an uneasy feeling. And his Dutch accent did sound very peculiar.

How could I not see it before?" She pounded her fists on her knees.

"Nobody could have seen it. I only worked it out because of Sherlock Holmes ... I mean, my book."

"Thank God for Sherlock Holmes, Katie. And thank God for you! But now I must tell you some terrible news which is even more terrible after what you've just told me."

I gulped. "Could anything be more terrible than things already are?"

"I fear they can." Sophia took a trembling breath to steady herself. I'd never seen her quite so shaken. "Last night the Baron called me to his chambers. He gave me an emerald necklace and told me it was a wedding present."

"A wedding present?" Now I was completely confused. "Whose wedding?"

"Mine."

I went from confused to dumbfounded. Sophia looked like she might be sick, but she bravely carried on. "The Baron never meant to marry the Countess. He wants much more than Otterly Manor and the Countess's lands. His plan was always to marry me and ally himself with the English and German Courts."

"But you're only a girl!" I squealed. "How can he marry a child?"

"According to our laws, I am nearly a woman, and old enough to be betrothed to a man. He says that the Countess has already agreed to the marriage, and it will take place immediately on the morrow so that the King and Queen can attend before the Court leaves Otterly Manor."

I felt the gruel I'd forced down that morning wanting to come back up. "But surely you don't *have* to marry him! You *can* say no …"

"That is the worst part." She grabbed my hand and clenched it. "The Baron made it unmistakably clear that if I refuse to marry him, there will be no way of saving Frederick. He said the necklace was only a token. The real wedding gift will be my brother's life. If I say no, Bessy will be hanged and Digby will be taken immediately to the Tower. His execution will take place just after the wedding tomorrow."

I was speechless and shivering uncontrollably.

Sophia's voice was hollow again. "This was the Baron's plot all along. He's orchestrated it perfectly, and there is nothing to be done about it. But at least there is something I can do. At least two innocent lives needn't be lost."

"No." I found my voice and looked Sophia in the eye. "You can't do it. You can't let that conniving murderer win."

"He won't win. Not entirely. After all, Frederick is still out there somewhere. If only I knew where! I have been praying he has escaped to make his way home to Germany. Our papa would raise an army, though it could mean our alliance with the English Court will be broken forever, and I will be lost to my family. Still—"

"I almost forgot!" I interrupted. "I just spoke with Jack Hornsby. He says Frederick is hidden somewhere nearby, though he wouldn't tell me where, and he's thinking of giving himself up to save Digby."

"He mustn't! Jack must see that he is chained up before letting him do a thing like that!"

"I'm afraid if he hears the Baron is forcing you to marry him, your brother would break through even the strongest chains."

Sophia pressed her palms together as if in prayer. "If only I could speak to him and beg him to take cover until he can return unseen to Germany! I can bear my marriage. I could not bear my brother's death."

My mind was racing again, groping for a solution, any solution! "Maybe *I* could speak to Frederick. If I could just persuade Jack to tell me his hiding place …"

"No, Katie." Sophia switched into her firm motherly self just like that.

"Why not?"

"I didn't want to say anything about it because the thought was too terrible, but before you discovered Master Van Hoebeek's true identity, when we thought he really was the murderer and had fled, I was worried that Tom might have fled with him, possibly never to return. That you might … well … "

"Be stuck here forever?" I finished for her.

She gave a solemn nod. "But now we know all of that was a tale, and the Baron is still right here at Otterly Manor. I believe Tom is very likely near as well. He wouldn't go far when the Baron has his daughter captive." She clasped my arm and looked firmly into my eyes. "Katie, you must find him and persuade him to send you home immediately. Life here under the Baron's control has become far too dangerous. Look at your hands." she turned over my palm, rope-burned from hauling water the day before. "You shouldn't have to suffer like this."

I pulled back my hand. One thing Sophia and I had in

common was our stubborn streaks. I wouldn't be so easily out-done. "Forget it, Sophia. I can't, I *won't* just leave you all in this muddle, even if I do find Tom. You said we have to make the most of our circumstances. Well you were right. I've come here for a reason, and I'm *going* to make the most of it by helping you and Frederick, and Digby and Bessy if I can."

Sophia gave me a wary look like she wanted to protest. But she had also given me an idea.

"Actually," — I tapped my lips, thinking — "you're right about Tom."

"So you'll look for him? You'll ask him to send you home?"

"I'll look for him, but what I'll ask him for is help. Like you said, the Baron has his daughter imprisoned. He can't have wanted to help a man like that. And yet … "

"He's been a part of the Baron's schemes from the start," Sophia finished.

"Exactly. So he might just be the one to help us find proof that the Baron is guilty."

"Yes! That is possible!" Sophia said with a flicker of hope.

"SOPHIAAA! MISTREEEES!" a lady's voice squawked over the cackle of chickens in the stable yard.

Sophia jumped to her feet. "Oh no. I have to go."

We hustled over to the ladder, and as Sophia gathered up her skirts and reached for the first rung, she stopped. "I don't know when we can meet again. Speak to Jack. Whatever else happens, he must stop Frederick from giving himself up!"

"I will," I promised, letting her hand slip from mine.

"But don't give up hope. We can still fight. There's still time to catch the Baron in his own game."

"You really are my guardian angel, Katie. God bless you, and grant you success!" She descended the ladder and waved a hurried goodbye from below. I waited until I heard her voice mingle with the lady's before I crept down the ladder myself. The first thing I had to do was find Jack Hornsby.

21

THE PAINTER'S WAGON

"*I* cannot. I swore on my life I would tell no living soul." Getting information out of Jack was proving more difficult than I'd anticipated.

"But Jack, this is a matter of life and death. If you won't tell me where Frederick is, then it's up to you. You *have* to keep him from coming out of his hiding place … at least until I can find Tom." I'd meant to say the last bit to myself, but Jack perked up.

"Tom? Tom did you say? Who d'you mean?"

He knew something about Tom. That much was obvious. "Tom the gypsy painter. He was working for Van Hoebeek. His daughter is the one accused of being the witch who aided Frederick in the Earl's murder."

"A lot of God-forsaken poppycock." Jack spat into the corner of the horse stall we had made into our secret consulting closet.

"Yes, it is. And if I find him, I may be able to prove it's all a lot of … you know."

"Poppycock?"

"Yeah. That."

Jack scratched his beard with twitchy fingers. He removed his hat and wiped his brow. I recognised the symptoms. He was having a debate with himself, and part of him wanted to help me.

"I reckon I never promised not to tell 'em where *he* was," he muttered to himself, the part of himself I was rooting for to win out. Then he nodded as if he'd come to his decision. "Alright, mistress. I can't tell you where Frederick is, but I can tell you that this Tom you're seeking, Tom Tippery, is here in the park, by the river. His place won't be easy to find — let's just say he's decorated it to match the forest — but look for smoke."

"Smoke?"

"That's all I can tell you, Mistress Katie."

"That's all I need!" I was so excited, I grabbed his hand and shook it. Without knowing it, he'd told me *exactly* where to find Tom. I lowered my head and rushed out of the stable, eager to be on my way to the ivy-covered shepherd's wagon I'd come across near the river.

But first, I needed my bag. If I was to run a proper interrogation on Tom Tippery, I would need my spy notebook; there was simply no going without it. But getting it was not going to be simple. After all, I was no longer free to wander the corridors of Otterly Manor. My place was the kitchen now, but getting to my room through the kitchen was hopeless — Mary Haye's would pin me down with duties the moment she saw me. I decided to risk suspicion by going around through the main gatehouse entrance as I'd always done as a chambermaid, through the courtyards, and into the Great Hall's main entrance. I walked past every servant I met with complete confidence, and, amazingly, nobody questioned me!

THE GREAT STAIRCASE brought me to the familiar old Portrait Gallery. There was not a soul around. I couldn't remember the exact panel Nurse Joan had opened in the wall, so I pushed on one after the other. Finally, the right one gave way. At the same time, I heard a *clop clop clop* at the end of the corridor and my heart leapt like a Mexican jumping bean. I pushed the panel open, threw myself inside and pushed it shut again, hoping against hope she hadn't seen me. Then, without looking back, I flew down the twisting stairway, down the dark corridor and into my room. The thought of Nurse Joan on my heels did me a favour by driving out all other fears. I threw on my backpack and ran right through the kitchen without even scanning for Mary Hayes, through the kitchen gardens, past the jail, and out into the open fields of the park.

I didn't stop to catch my breath until I was well down the sloping dirt carriageway and out of sight from the house.

After four journeys to the river, my feet knew the way without needing to consult my brain. That's probably why I was too deep in thought imagining how my conversation with Tom would go to notice the earth rumbling beneath me and the swelling clamour of dogs howling. Not until a bushy white stag plunged out of the bracken and halted in the road right in front of me did I become aware. The stag stopped just long enough to give me a wild look that seemed to mean "Run!" Then he bound into the under-growth on the other side of the road.

I stood frozen like a deer in the headlights. The rumble of hooves and yelps of the dogs sounded as if they were heading right for me. I felt like *I* was being hunted. My brain went blank except for that one word: *Run!*

Down the hill, zipping through birch trees, I didn't look back, but I felt them getting closer. I could hear men's shouts now. The Baron's voice calling "Halloo ahead!", the swoosh of bracken being ripped up by an army of hungry hounds. I couldn't outrun them, so I slid into a hollow made by vines growing thick over a tall bush. I ducked down in the bracken and waited, my heart and lungs in flames.

In a minute, the yelping was so close it made my ears ring. Then it was sniffing. A chorus of sniffing noses so close their breath made the hairs on the back of my neck stand up. *Sniff … sniff sniff.* Then *WOOooooo!* The hound over me let out a howl that made my teeth chatter. I clasped my hands over my ears and clenched my eyes shut, wondering if the Baron or the King would be the one to mistake me for a deer and shoot me. After all, if something so intelligent as a dog could make such a mistake, there was no hope the Baron wouldn't. Or maybe the dog just smelled the ball in my backpack.

The ball! I let go of my ears and tore my bag off my back. As the earth quaked with hooves trampling down the hill, I pulled out my only weapon: Oscar's plastic ball sling. I took careful aim, and fired.

The hound over my head went silent. His sharp eyes followed the ball's curve, far away across the hillside; then he lunged after it with every passionate muscle in his canine body. The rest of the pack sprinted after him, and soon the thunder of the hunting party's horses died away as the Baron, the King and all the King's men pursued old Oscar's tennis ball.

I had to laugh when I reached the river and found my fellow prey, the white stag, enjoying a relaxed drink. "Looks like we both outsmarted them this time." He raised his head to me, which I took as a "thank you". So I curt-seyed back to him, and we went our separate ways, he slipping through the curtain of bracken and I turning right towards the ivy-covered shepherd's wagon where a thin ribbon of smoke promised someone was home.

The little glade where the wagon was tucked away was so quiet, my own footsteps might as well have been alarm bells. Every cracking twig, every crunching beechnut echoed. Even so, I did my best to creep up on the scene, not wanting to give Tom a chance to lock himself inside and hide away from me. I pressed my back against the long, vine-covered side of the wagon and inched along its length until I inched myself around the corner. I had been looking behind me, making sure I wasn't being followed, so when a puff of hot breath blew against the back of my head and neck, a scream caught in my throat and I threw my arms over my head. Thankfully (or I'd have given away Tom's location to the entire hunting party) I choked on the scream. The thing was, that blast of breath felt so familiar, I didn't even need to look to know where it had come from. I could picture the two fleshy nostrils in my mind's eye. I smiled, relieved, and lowered my arms to find, just as I'd expected, a horse gazing back at me. Not just any horse. Vagabond.

He pawed at the earth and whinnied under his breath, agitated. "Shhhh. You're alright. You're safe," I whispered. Without even thinking twice, I reached out my hand to stroke his neck, then remembered what Digby had said about the horse being a biter. I held out my hand to him, palm up. He smelled it and lowered his head, his nose nuzzling my shoulder, and I knew he wasn't going to bite me. When I laid my hand against his warm hide, it felt like magic. My fingers glided over the two raised scars as I stroked Vagabond's strong neck. "No wonder you're angry. How could they do this to you? And how on earth did Jack get you down here?"

"Hornsby said you sent him."

I gasped and spun around. There behind me, never making the slightest peep, sat Tom Tippery at his easel with a brush in one hand and a little wooden box of paints on his knee. I laid my hand on my chest to stop my heart from its sudden tap dance.

Tom smiled softly, almost timidly. "He only arrived some moments before you did. Still settling, I think. You're the first person I've seen stroke him like that." He paused to dab his brush into the box, carrying on with his business. "It's Katherine, is it not?"

I was still searching for words and breath, so I nodded. "And you're Tom?" I muttered.

He gave me another kindly smile and dip of the head, then returned to his painting. After a few brush strokes, he propped his brush hand down on his knee and looked at his picture, thoughtfully cocking his head to one side and fingering the small hoop earring he wore in one ear. "I'm not sure I've really captured it. Would you care to have a look?"

For the second time since coming to the wagon, I found to my surprise that I felt completely at ease. Tom sounded so gentle, like a bashful young boy, and his eyes had a sad puppy quality about them. Here sat a sad, lonely man whose daughter's life was now in danger. And what could he do but sit there and paint? I was sure Tom, like Vagabond, meant me no harm.

The dying fire crackled as I stepped closer to him to look over his shoulder at the canvas. The last bit of breath went out of me when I saw what was on it. "It's the painting," I breathed. "The one that brought me here." It was all there just as I'd remembered it: the park with its rolling hills and forests, the tiny hunting party in the distance, the big black horse beside the wagon, and Tom hunched over his canvas, his eyes twinkling in the sun rays that crept through the tree branches. And there was the strawberry-haired girl I had wished was me. I half-smiled to myself, still bewildered as it dawned on me: it *was* me the whole time.

"How did you do it?" I asked. "It's not … you know … black magic, is it?"

Tom stood up and walked around me to poke the fire with a stick. "I'm no saint, Mistress Katherine. But I read the Scriptures and commit my soul to the Almighty. This —" he waved his hand at the canvas — "this is God's gift, not the devil's … though I cannot claim innocence for having never sold God's gift to the devil," he mumbled into the fire.

"You mean the Baron?" I had now completely forgotten the spy notebook I'd risked so much to get and my carefully pre-planned investigation questions. Now, I just genuinely wanted to know how someone so ordinary and seemingly kind — just as Sophia had said — could take part in such a dark, horrible plot. "But why? Why would you help him murder someone and take all the credit for your work at the same time? It doesn't make sense."

Tom rubbed his scruffy chin as he gazed into the fire. He seemed to be struggling with himself, almost in tears even. He looked at me timidly with the flicker of a sad smile. "It does looks grave, does it not? But in fact, it's worse than you think. I didn't just paint for the Baron." He picked up his box of paints and plodded up a step ladder to the wagon's door, opened it and disappeared inside. Was I supposed to follow? I took a few uncertain steps forward.

Tom's messy grey head poked out of the door a moment later. "Please, won't you come in?"

He held the door open for me. I hesitated a moment pondering what might be inside that wagon. Someone who'd rescued a condemned horse could not be dangerous, I decided, and stepped boldly up the ladder.

Whatever I'd expected to find inside, it was not in a hundred years what met my eyes. The walls were lined with trunks, and above those were pegs, each holding the oddest, most dazzling assortment of clothes: jewel spangled velvets, peacock feathers, fairy wings and enough frills and lace to dress the entire King's Court! Strung across the ceiling were hooks with every sort of hat, mask or headpiece imaginable: mesh horse faces, soldier's helmets, jester's hats, wild white wigs and a whole string of fake beards. I reached up above my head and rubbed one of the wigs between my thumb and finger. It felt just like sheep's wool.

"Very observant of you," Tom said over his shoulder. He was washing his paint-stained hands in a water basin when I turned around. "It is identical to the one the Baron wore with *his* disguise as Master Van Hoebeek. But of course you have worked it out for yourself." He dried his hands on a rag and gestured to a stool in a snug sitting space between the racks of costumes. I sat, and so did he. He offered me some dried apricots, then lit up a pipe, took a few puffs of it, and eased back into his story.

"You see, Mistress Katherine, I'm not a true artist. I make my living as a travelling mask maker. I've been invited to many a great house, and even to Court when there is a masquerade or a theatrical performance to supply for. But once the masque is over, I'm sent away, my craft forgotten." He smiled sadly again. "I've always dreamt of becoming a real court painter. A master even. Then I'd be able to give my Bessy a proper home … a cottage where she could raise chickens, grow herbs." He pulled off his cloth cap and wiped his brow. I detected his chin quivering ever so slightly. With a cracking voice, he continued. "And now, thanks to my greed, what I've earned for her instead is a prison cell."

To see an old man filled with regret and on the brink of tears made me feel so sorry for him, I wanted to reach out. I tried to sound caring rather than accusing when I asked, "But how did it happen? How did you begin working for the Baron?"

Taking another puff of his pipe, Tom squinted as if to see into the past. "I said the nobility forgot me and my craft, but not the Baron. I supplied the masks for his ball last spring. He came personally to my wagon to look at my collection of costumes, but when he saw my paintings, he asked if I had any interest in a commission as an assistant court painter. And, of course, I had. He told me a little of his plan — he wanted to infiltrate his brother's house for information. I knew deception would be involved, but it seemed nothing more than another masquerade to me then."

I watched Tom closely. His eyes stared into nothing, fixed on something only he could see. He continued. "When at last I discovered the sinister nature of the Baron's plot, I professed I wanted no more part in it. But I was too late. He had already taken Bessy. He locked her away and swore she'd burn as a witch unless I saw the job through and told not a soul. If he knew I told you this tale now …" His eyes darted nervously towards the door, then fell back to his lap. He sighed, and slumped over like an old dog. "I know not what to do."

I had come to Tom looking for hope. It seemed hope was the very thing Tom needed too. But what hope could *I* offer? The Baron had us all tied up and chained to his plan. I just sat there in silence.

The silence was shattered by a sudden, explosive *AaaaCHEEEW!*

I jumped to my feet. "What was that?"

Tom's eyes were fixed anxiously on a curtain just behind me that separated a smaller area of the wagon from the main room.

AaaaCHEEEW! It came again. I knew that sneeze.

"No, don't ..." Tom stood and reached out his arm to stop me, but he was too late. I yanked back the curtain. There was a straw mat on the floor, and above my eye level, reclined in a sort of loft, was a bear. It startled me at first, until I understood what it *really* was: Frederick holding a bear mask over his face. I could still see his eyes through the holes in the mask, and they gave the bear a sheepish expression.

I stared in amazement, not knowing what to say except the obvious: "Bless you."

22

THE PLAN

"So, wait. You've been hiding here the whole time, ever since the banquet?" I asked the boy with the bear face.

Frederick took off his mask and climbed down from the loft. "Hornsby came to warn me about what had happened to the Earl, and that Van Hoebeek had accused me and Bessy of conspiring the whole thing. When I heard Digby had been arrested in my place, I wanted to give myself up then and there. But Hornsby rightly made me see that my coming forward would not save Digby from danger. As long as I was free, there was hope of putting things right ... somehow." The muscles in Frederick's square jaw twitched. "Jack didn't know where to hide me, though. Luckily, we met Tom in the park. He explained Van Hoebeek's true identity and that his daughter was caught in the Baron's web as well. He offered to hide me here, where I could think ... make a plan."

"It was the least I could do, considering how much of that web was my own spinning," Tom muttered from his stool where he'd begun whittling away at some sort of flute.

"You're not to blame, Tom. No more than I am. Sophia was the wise one. Had I only accepted my duty and chosen to make the most of it rather than gratifying my whims, Digby would be free this day. The fool I was!" He pounded his fist against the wall, causing the wagon to rock like a boat.

I stumbled and threw my hand out to catch my balance, which must've drawn Frederick's attention. "Katie, what are you wearing?" he asked with a tinge of worry.

I looked down at my mud-smudged apron and linen frock. "New clothes?" I offered. But Frederick was too quick to have the wool pulled over his eyes. He knew right away something was up.

"Where is Sophia? Is she safe? Has the Baron turned her into a kitchen wench as well?"

"No ..." I hesitated.

"Tell me, Katie." He looked almost dangerous. "How is my sister?"

I took a deep breath and blew it out slowly, bracing myself for the storm I knew would break loose the moment I spoke. "She is safe, but ... Just after the Baron arrived ... I mean, just after he stopped pretending to be Master Van Hoebeek, he separated us. He gave Sophia some of his own ladies to wait on her, though I'm sure it was really to spy on her and make sure she didn't get up to anything."

"And the Baron sent you off to the servant's quarters?"

I nodded.

"Then you haven't seen her?"

"No. Yes, I mean. I have. Just this morning we met in the hayloft while everybody else was busy sending off the hunting party."

"And she is well?"

"She *is* well, but ..."

"But? But what?" Frederick took a step closer. His eyes flickered with electricity.

There was no hiding the truth. I spat it out in one breath. "The Baron is forcing Sophia to marry him in exchange for Digby's life ... *your* life."

I watched my words sink in. A deep red flush crept up Frederick's neck and into his cheeks. His nostrils flared with every fuming breath. Then the explosion. I winced as he drew a long sword out of a scabbard hanging from the loft and pushed passed me with the force of a hurricane.

"The Baron shall wed Sophia over my dead body!" He growled.

"Yes!" Tom stood in Frederick's way with his hand outstretched. "That is exactly how he shall wed her if you rush out in this manner."

Frederick lowered his voice but spoke through clenched teeth. "Let me pass, Tom, or I shall have no choice but to remove you."

"Tom's right!" I shouted. "And anyway, Sophia will never forgive you if you go and get yourself killed." I noticed Tom's Adam's apple jump. His daughter's life was at stake here as well. "And don't forget Digby and Bessy," I added. "Do you really think you can save them by turning yourself in?"

"I won't turn myself in. I'll kill the Baron."

Tom grabbed Frederick's sword hand and wrenched the weapon out of it. "Then you'll be hanged for sure."

"So you two would have me sit here, safely holed away, while others pay the price? While that bloody Baron makes a slave of my sister?"

"No." I felt a confidence that amazed even me. This was my time to live up to the name Watson. To make Charlie proud, if he could only see me. "We'll save Sophia together, the three of us. And Bessy." I looked to Tom who cast me another sad but grateful smile. "And Digby as well. But we can't do it without a plan. What we need is hard, cold evidence to prove that the Baron is guilty. Tom?"

Tom crossed his arms and stroked his chin in deep thought. "The Baron has hidden his effects within Otterly Manor. He keeps them all in a trunk: his disguise, the bottle of poison he used to kill the Earl, and the draught he's giving the Countess to keep her in a stupor until he deems it safe to kill her as well. I have also seen there a stash of letters from his mistress in Chudleigh expressing her impatience to come and live at Otterly Manor once he has married the 'little German Princess'."

Frederick let out a growl, but Tom continued. "It's all there, safely tucked out of sight."

"You've seen all that in Otterly Manor?" I asked. "But where could he hide it that nobody would see?"

"Can you not guess?" Tom winked at me, just as he had from the painting a lifetime ago. So that was it.

"It's hidden in the secret room where I saw your painting, isn't it." Tom winked again. "So that's why the Baron as Van Hoebeek didn't like me going near it. *And* he hung his own portrait over the panel. What a snob!"

Frederick looked between the two of us, confused. "There's a secret room in Otterly Manor?"

"It's off the Billiard Gallery, behind a fake panel," I explained. Then, turning back to Tom, asked, "And you're sure all of that stuff is there?"

He looked down. "The Baron locked Bessy away in that room on the night of the banquet. I was permitted to go into the chamber to speak to her one last time, to tell her it would be alright. To lie." He paused. "I saw everything I've mentioned there that night."

"Then we've got to get in there."

"I'll go," Frederick blurted.

"Frederick!" I snapped. "You can't go in there!"

"It is *my* house!" He beat himself on the chest just like a male gorilla.

"Yes, I know it is, but your waltzing in there would ruin everything! The house has been crawling with the King's guards ever since the Earl was murdered. You'd be arrested in no time, which would defeat the purpose of making THIS PLAN, REMEMBER?"

"Yes," he said, again through gritted teeth.

Boys, I thought. "It only makes sense for me to go. I'm still a part of the household. As long as I steer clear of Nurse Joan … and Mary Hayes … and probably Anna, nobody will think twice about my being in the house. I could go during supper when the gallery is deserted."

Frederick and Tom exchanged an uncertain look. I guess neither of them liked the idea of sending a little girl into danger's way instead of going in himself. But we all knew it was the best way of getting the evidence without our plan being found out, and we all agreed we *had* to get that evidence tonight. After all, there was no time to lose. The wedding — not to mention the execution — was set for tomorrow.

Tom nodded first, then Frederick. "Supper it is then," the younger man said running his fingers through his blonde hair.

The only thing to do then was the thing I'd grown to hate most: wait. It wasn't even noon yet. The hunting party would still be out in the park — we could still hear the dogs baying. Supper wouldn't be served before six. That's when I would make my move.

23

LAST HOPE

I didn't go back to the kitchens all day, but stayed hidden away at Tom's wagon along with Frederick and Vagabond. Tom reckoned I'd get a good scolding if I went back, and Mary Hayes would keep me doubly busy so I was sure not to wander off. And then there was the hunting party I didn't care to run into *again*. I only had one more tennis ball to spare! But not going back did mean my task would be even more dangerous. I was now a runaway servant, shirking my duties. Mary may already have reported me to Nurse Joan, and she would have her hawk eyes on the lookout for me. She might even speak to the Baron about me once he returned to the house.

"Maybe I should wear one of your beards when I go back, so no one will recognise me," I joked to Tom while he stirred a stew over the fire. I was trying to ease my own nerves.

But instead of laughing, he looked thoughtful. "I could paint on a sprinkling of pox boils here and there. That way if anybody gives you trouble, they'll at least believe you were ill in truth … and they are like to jump away from you faster than a jack rabbit."

"Or maybe throw me out of the house faster than a jack rabbit," I laughed, holding my palm out to Vagabond so he could nibble up the carrot stalks I'd collected for him from Tom's chopping block.

Tom glanced up. "That horse is a different beast in your presence."

"He reminds me of my horse back home, Gypsy," I said, but of course that wasn't quite true. "Or, at least he used to be my horse." And somehow, just like that, I was telling Tom Tippery everything — about my accident and how I hadn't been able to mount a horse ever since, about Charlie going off to university, about all the things that used to worry me so much. But it was all so far away. "It's strange, but now all of that stuff sounds so silly and unimportant. I always wanted someone else's life … an exciting one, like Sophia's. But now that I know what it's like, I miss my old life. My family. I guess I had it pretty good after all."

"I think …" Tom began without looking up from his stew, "we all find ourselves in circumstances we wouldn't choose at times. But still we have a choice." He looked up and smiled. "What to make of them. We can choose courage. Responsibility. Truth." He clacked the spoon against the pot and sat down on a log. "I chose cowardice. Now others are paying the price."

"But your daughter's life was in danger. Who could blame you?"

Tom shook his head. "I should have trusted in God

rather than fearing the Baron. Then I might have found help."

I moved over to sit on the stump beside Tom's. "It's not too late. You can still find help." I felt it sounded a little hollow, but Tom smiled with what looked like genuine gratitude.

"You know, Mistress Katherine, there is one thing I do not regret, and that is bringing you here. Were times less dire, I should like to hear all about the world you come from." He sighed. "Suffice it to say, you have served many here. May your time here serve you as well."

We sat silently for a minute, then the question that had become buried under the day's events bubbled up to the surface once again. "You know, Tom, you still haven't told me how you did it. How you brought me here. If it wasn't black magic, then …"

Tom smiled. "I will show you." He got up and went into the wagon, then came back a second later carrying his wooden box of paints. "Here. Have a look." He held out the box to me.

I took it and looked at the carving on its top. It was of a face hidden in a ring of oak leaves. A Green Man like the one on the trick panel. I ran my fingers over the face and heard a latch click. Inside the box were two rows of three pots, each one filled with a different colour paint. I'd done enough of art class to know there was something definitely peculiar about these paints. The colours had a sort of shimmering silver sheen to them, and they moved. Though I held the box perfectly still on my knees, the paints swirled non-stop in their pots like living creatures. "What kind of paints *are* these?" I asked, unable to stop watching the colours perform their whirlpool movement.

"I bought them from an old woman I happened to meet at a travelling fair. She told me they were magic paints, and claimed that when the onlooker beheld in a painting his deepest desire, the paints possessed the power to give him the thing that would content his heart."

I thought about that for a minute. "When I looked at the painting, I wished for a different life. One with more excitement and adventure."

He took the box from me and closed it gently. "I didn't truly believe her at the time. I only thought the pigments were interesting and wondered what effect they might make on a canvas. But I suppose a bit of curiosity lingered. So I painted myself as a court painter, drawing the portraits of the nobility. No sooner was that picture done, the Baron offered me a commission. So I thought just maybe ..."

A horrible thought occurred to me. "Does the Baron know about these paints?"

Tom shook his head. "I never told him, nor did I use them to paint any of the Baron's commissioned portraits. I had enough sense at least to know that such power, if truly power there were, could be put to terrible purposes. Once I discovered the Baron's true intentions, I intended to destroy the paints. But first I decided it could not do much harm to give them one last try ... This time not for my own ends, but for the sake of someone whose heart's desire was something pure and simple."

"Sophia," I said. "She told you she wanted a friend."

"Yes."

My mind churned over everything Tom had just been telling me. "So then, when Sophia looked into the painting, she saw a friend. And when I looked, hundreds of years later, I saw myself in a different life."

"And when I looked," — He sat so we were knee-to-knee and face-to-face — "I saw our last hope."

I looked up into Tom's earnest, fatherly eyes. "So you really do think I'm here for a purpose? That I'll be able to help change all this somehow? I mean, it *will* take a miracle."

He placed his rough hand gently over mine where they lay folded on my knees. "You're here, aren't you? Miracles happen."

CLOSE CALLS AND BAD NEWS

*A*s the hours ticked on, the sky grew dark. By five o'clock when it was nearly time to go, the wagon quivered in the whipping wind and a slanting rain drummed on its wooden sides.

We'd spent the last hour sitting all together in the wagon, eating Tom's stew and working out the details of our plan. Supper was the best time to go unseen into the Billiard Gallery, but by far the worst time to trudge through the Great Hall or the kitchens to get there. Luckily, Frederick knew of a back entrance that would take me through an outer passage into the Water Court where I'd find a turret staircase that opened up right into the Billiard Gallery.

Frederick pointed to the gate on the map he'd sketched for me on a bit of spare fabric. "The guards change at six o'clock. The gate will open on the hour to let the new guards out and the old ones in for supper. That will be your chance to slip through and hide until the gates close again and the old guards are out of earshot."

My palms became increasingly sweaty as he spoke. "Erm ... right. How exactly am I to sneak past four guards without getting caught again?"

Frederick sat back and sighed. Not the encouraging answer I'd have liked.

But Tom, who'd been listening, silently stroking his whiskers, leaned in to have a look at the map. "I think I can help you there. A little distraction is all you need to slip through undetected."

"But Tom, you can't! You mustn't be seen. The Baron ..."

He stopped me with his raised hand. "*I* won't be seen." He stood up and rummaged among the costumes a moment before snatching down a long, white beard from a hook on the wall. He turned his back to us as he fitted it over his face. When he turned back, he had transformed before our eyes into an old man twice his own age at least.

"Let me go, Tom. I can don a disguise as well as you can," Frederick insisted.

But Tom shook his head. "My boy, you are the Earl of Otterly Manor. Much depends upon you. I on the other hand ... disguise is what I do."

Frederick looked flustered, but it was clear that Tom had made up his mind. He completed his costume with a broad-brimmed, floppy hat, a long cloak and a walking cane. I was sure I wouldn't have known him if I'd passed him in the park.

It was still pouring, or *chucking it down* as my mum would say, so Tom rummaged around in a trunk and found a sealskin cloak with a hood that fit me perfectly. The last thing was for Tom to paint on my pox. He did only three — two on my forehead and one on my chin. "We do not want you to look like a ladybird," he said, standing back to examine his artistry.

And then it was time to brave the rain and, more dangerously, to brave the many, watchful eyes in Otterly Manor. We heard the distant tower clock chime half past five, said goodbye to Frederick who wished us Godspeed, put up our cloaks and plunged into the downpour. We passed Vagabond, stood out of the rain beneath the wagon's little awning. He whinnied, as if to ask where I was going. I patted his shoulder. "I'll be back," I promised.

WE DIDN'T SPEAK on the whole long trudge up the hill. The rain beat down too heavily and we both kept our hoods pulled low over our faces. We had to walk fast if we hoped to get to the gate at a minute before six.

At five minutes before the hour, we reached the house. Though Tom's hood was drawn up, I saw him cast a longing look towards the prison.

I leaned over so he could hear me. "I'll do my best in there," I said. "For Bessy."

We inched along the stone wall, listening out for any straggler servants returning late from the hay threshing. But the rain had driven everyone indoors. Everyone, that is, except the guards. We were just a pebble's throw from the end of the wall, which meant that right around the corner, the two guards stood post.

Tom squinted against the rain to peer at the clock tower. "'It is time," he mouthed. "Get ready." And just like that, he scuffled out into the open, all hunched over and dragging one leg behind him.

"Who goes there?" I heard a guard shout.

Tom spun around and shouted in a strange, wiry voice nothing like his normal soft one. "Greetings, young sire. I am the noble Francis Drake. I sailed the seas for Her Majesty Queen Elizabeth and am come here to receive my reward from her hand. Will you lead me to her?" He dipped down in a clumsy bow and rose up again with a whoosh of his cape.

"Alright. Move along. There's no Queen Bess here, *Sir Francis Drake*. Either you've had a few too many pints of ale, or you've lost your wits somewhere on the road."

"Ale, did he say?" Tom put a hand to his ear.

At the same time, the clock struck six and the bell began to toll. Just as Frederick had said, the gate screeched open. I inched a little closer to the corner and peeked around. Four men in breastplates and helmets who looked just like the three musketeers and d'Artagnan clustered together at the open gate.

"You're free to sup, you two," a deep voice said.

"Thank heavens! We shall leave you two to deal with this." The guard thumbed over his shoulder towards Tom who was doing a funny little hobbling jig in the road. "Think his pot is a bit cracked, if you know what I mean."

All four of them turned their attention to Tom, and I knew with a flutter of my heart that this was my one and only chance. I crouched low and ran, close to the wall, on my tip-toes, and I didn't look around to see if the guards noticed until I was through the gate. There was the stone passage — a sort of corridor under an arched roof. I

181

crouched behind a statue of a woman with a bow and arrows and waited, trying very hard to quiet the noisy duet between my breath and my heart.

In barely no time at all — it made me feel faint to think what a close call it had been — the voices of the two old guards echoed against the stone passage walls. "If he gives them any trouble, they'll just lock him away with the witch and the little traitor, and we can have a triple execution on the morrow," the first one said.

"I thought the young Earl was destined for the Tower? Devil worshiper or not, he is nobility."

"I had it from the Baron's chief guardsman this morning," the second guard answered. "Both the Earl and the witch are to be hanged just as soon as the Baron returns from his wedding, around midday."

"What, before the wedding feast?" asked the other. "Seems an odd way to commence a banquet ..."

"Nah, the banquet guests won't even know the execution's taken place; it's to happen quietly. The Baron's ordered they do it as soon as they hear the church bells toll, signifying the wedding's over."

I strained my ears, but I couldn't hear another word after that. Once the two guardsmen passed my hiding place, their voices were drowned by the burbling of the fountain in the middle of the Water Court, which was overflowing after the downpour. I let out the breath I'd been holding, but it came out as shiver. I knew the Baron was evil, but I could not believe he had lied to Sophia to persuade her to marry him without a fuss. She *would* marry him, but all for nothing: it would not save Digby or Bessy from hanging.

For a moment, I just crouched in the shadow, paralysed. So much depended on me getting into that room and back out again without being caught. Lives depended on it. Messing up was not an option. I took a few deep breaths, then clenched my eyes shut and prayed just one word: "Help."

Just then, the dark rain clouds broke up and evening sun rays spilled into the stone passage, making glistening mists of the puddles. The warm sunlight filled my veins with fresh courage. I pulled up my cloak and walked — running would have alerted suspicion — to the outer stair.

It was right where Frederick's map had said it would be. I wound my way up, balancing myself with one hand against the cold stone wall, until I came to a narrow wooden door at the top. I pulled the map out from my apron pocket and, using a candle from a wall sconce, I took stock of where I was. According to the map, this door would bring me out into the Billiard Room, which opened right up into the Billiard Gallery. I was mere steps away from the secret chamber.

I pressed my ear against the door. Not a sound. *All the waiting servants must be at dinner by now*, I thought. So I turned the doorknob and pushed the door open just a crack. Still nothing stirred. I stepped into the Billiard Room and inched along the wall, trying with difficulty to walk silently on the wooden floorboards. I only needed to turn a sharp right and I would be in the Green Man's corner, in the very spot where I'd been whisked away into the past … the very spot where the Baron, dressed as Van Hoebeek, had sneaked up on me and nearly scared me to death … Why was it things always happened in that spot?

I stretched out my neck and peered down the whole length of the Billiard Gallery. Nothing moved but dust motes drifting on evening sunbeams. I had the clear. I turned the corner, came face-to-face with the old Green Man, reached up my hand, laid it on his leafy face and …

Creeeak. Like déjà vu, the panel crept open. I glanced around one last time and stepped inside.

25

CAUGHT

*G*ood thing I'd taken that candle. The room's slit window faced east, away from the setting sun. But for my candle beam, dusky darkness filled the chamber and the few objects inside appeared like creepy black blobs.

I pulled the door closed all but a crack behind me — after all, I had never got out of the room before, and the last thing I wanted now was to get myself locked in. Holding the candle up above my eyes, the light fell on a pile of rectangular objects propped against the wall. I moved closer and recognised the Baron's easel and a stack of blank canvases. Evidence all right, but not quite the evidence I needed. I straightened up and peered around the room looking for the trunk.

There was a chair, a chamber pot and, *aha!* There was the trunk. Best of all, when I knelt down to try the lock, it was open! The Baron clearly never expected anyone to discover his hiding place.

"Come on. Come on. Come on," I whispered to the trunk as I lifted the lid and held my breath, hoping with all my might the Baron hadn't removed the evidence since Tom had seen it.

"Yes!" I almost laughed with relief when I held up the candle and found the trunk full. Wrapped up in a painter's smock, I found a skull cap with the stringy brown wig attached to it and none other than the black woolly beard that had given Baron Black Sheep's false identity away. Beneath that was a corked bottle labelled *Property of Baron Buckville* in cursive script. At the bottom of everything I found a stack of letters tied together with a red ribbon.

With my one free hand, I managed to undo the bow and unfold the first letter. It was slow work. Whoever wrote these letters had the most spindly writing imaginable. But what I could make out was the *Your Faithful* at the end, and some sort of list of ingredients for a recipe called *Inheritance Powder*. But it must have been a very strange recipe from what I could make out of the ingredients, things like monk's blood, nightshade berries and even frogs' eyes! I winced at the thought of whatever concoction *these* items whipped up.

I folded the letter back up. I would take the stack to Tom and let him decipher the spindly words. There was no sense in struggling through the rest of them now; the sooner I got back to the wagon, the sooner Tom, Frederick and I could sort through the evidence and make our plan of attack on the Baron.

I packed away all the contents of the trunk in my backpack and zipped it up with a feeling of satisfaction. I could not wait to see the look on the Baron's face when we proved before the King that he was a cold-blooded murderer. I blew out my candle, slung my bag onto my back and covered it with my cloak then crept to the door to listen. Still no sound of any living creature, but I did hear the bell toll for the half-hour, which meant the household had been served their supper and now the kitchen staff would be having theirs in the Great Hall. Now I'd be able to slip through the hidden door in the Portrait Gallery and take the servant's passage to the kitchens to freedom and safety. Everything was working to plan.

But I still had the whole stretch of the Billiard Gallery to walk down first. It felt horribly exposed. With my heart in my throat, I speed-walked across the creaky floorboards, checked the little passage with the window, and made it undetected into the Portrait Gallery. A quick look up and down it told me I was safe to hop across the hall to the hidden door.

This time I knew which panel to push right away. I laid my hands on it and gave a gentle push. Just as it gave way, something wrenched me backwards by my cloak hood. Choking on what might have been my loudest scream ever, I looked up into the hateful eyes and triumphant sneer of Nurse Joan.

With one icy hand, she pulled back my head, and she pinched my ear with the other so that I winced in pain. The stench of her rotten breath in my face nearly gagged me.

"I knew you were a peck o'trouble from the moment you appeared in this house like an ill omen," she snarled.

"I see what you are. Strange ways, devil-kissed hair. You brought these misfortunes on us, *witch!*" She spat the word, spraying my face. "First the Earl drops dead. And my poor mistress would be cold in the grave beside him were it not for the Baron's medicinal brews keeping her on the other side of death's door."

"It's poison!" I screamed through teeth gritted in fear and pain.

"Quiet!" she spat again, giving my head another hard wrench. "I'll not hear another word of your lies. I knew I should've warned my mistress of you that first day, before you had the chance to wreak your wicked ways on this noble house. I'll not make that mistake this time. I'll see the Baron deals with you just as soon as he returns from his wedding." With that she pushed me forward into the stairwell with a jab of her knee. All the way down I struggled and screamed, "I'm not a witch! It's the Baron! The Baron is poisoning the Countess! It's a trick!" But every word only won me another shove or an even harder yank on my hair.

I had one last hope. "I have the pox!" I screamed. "Look!"

That made her stop and stare at my face with uncertain eyes. "I know what those are." Her voice was low. Hushed. "Witch's marks. You filthy, vile creature!" My hair got the hardest yank yet.

Tears blurred my eyes so that I couldn't tell which way we walked at the bottom of the stair, but the ground felt like it was sloping downward, and then we were walking down more narrow stairs. At last she pulled me to a halt by my hair, jammed a key into a large wooden door, pushed it open and flung me inside so hard I fell, my knees smacking cold, hard stone.

"You'll end up just like all your kind. Mark my words." And with that the door slammed. The lock clicked. Nurse Joan's clopping footsteps died away.

My whole body was shaking, either from shock or because the room was so cold, I don't know which. I struggled to my feet and rubbed my sore knees. Whatever the place was, it had a very unpleasant, sour smell and it was as black as ink. There was not even a thread of light beneath the door. But I could tell from the echoing sound of my breath it was a big room. I held my hands out in front of me and scuffed my feet forward, groping for a piece of furniture or the wall. I just wanted to feel near something rather than stranded in the middle of dark, endless space. My hand brushed against something. I reached out and the thing moved away, then back. It brushed my hands again. I pulled them back, panting with fright, then swallowed and reached out again, this time grabbing the thing.

It was soft one way and rough the other, like a dog's fur. A sickening idea came into my mind. I moved my hands along and felt what I'd feared: ears, a head, a leathery nose, long legs and hooves. It was a deer. And hanging beside it were others. Of all the ghastly places, Nurse Joan had locked me away in the meat cellar! No one would hear me if I screamed. No one would come looking for me. And by the time Nurse Joan let me out to face the Baron, it would be too late.

I crawled on my hands and knees across the straw-strewn floor until I found the wall. Wrapping my cloak tightly around me and hugging my knees close to my chest, I closed my eyes and tried to remember the family I might never see again. Nan and Pop, Mum, Dad, Charlie … Like painting portraits in my mind, I pictured every detail of their faces, over and over and over again until the pictures faded away and my mind became blank.

26

AN AUDIENCE WITH THE QUEEN

*M*y eyes opened but I saw nothing. My bones ached of long hours spent on a cold, hard surface. That ache brought the memory of where I was rushing over me like ice cold water. Hunger gnawed at my empty stomach, but at the same time, the smell of dead things made me want to be sick. I didn't know how long I'd slept or what time of day it was. By now Sophia might already be married to the Baron, and Digby and Bessy might be hanging in the courtyard. That thought really did make me retch, but there was nothing inside me to throw up, so I heaved and coughed instead.

I clenched my stomach and groaned, letting my weight flop back against the wall. Then I froze. Something rattled in the direction of the door. Someone was opening it. But that meant … Nurse Joan had said she would come for me after the Baron's wedding. So it was done. I had failed.

Sickness overcame me, and I doubled over heaving just before the door swung open. I picked myself up and scrambled to get my backpack on beneath my cloak. I wouldn't give it up any sooner than I had to. I heard heavy, scuffling footsteps coming towards me — definitely not Nurse Joan's clopping ones. But after an eternity in the pitch black, I couldn't see. I had to shield my eyes from the candlelight that was growing closer with each footstep.

"She's over there," I heard Nurse Joan's unmistakable, sharp voice snap from the doorway. Then large, gruff hands grabbed me under my arms and hoisted me up like I was a rag doll. "Make her walk," Nurse Joan commanded. Before I could put one foot in front of the other, one of the big hands took hold of my forearm in a killer grip and yanked me forward.

I felt too sick, both in my stomach and in my heart, to fight. My eyes were still adjusting to the little bit of candle-light. Even if I could escape the big man who had me by the arm, I wouldn't get far, blind and lost as I was. So I scuttled along as he dragged me to keep up with Nurse Joan's clopping gait.

After we'd walked up more stairs and down more corridors than I could keep up with, Nurse Joan came to a halt in front of a set of carved double doors. "I have had it from the steward that there is to be a hanging today." I wasn't sure whether she spoke to me or my guard. "The Baron, I am certain, will want to be rid of all you vermin in one go." And with that she straightened up and knocked on the door.

A steward with the royal crest embroidered on his chest opened it. Only then did I understand that we were in the Royal Chambers.

Nurse Joan made a curt curtsey. "I wish to speak to the Baron immediately. 'Tis a matter of grave importance ... of *treason.*" She looked just like an old vulture with her eyes bulging out.

The steward looked sceptically at the big man gripping my shoulder and then down at me. "I'm afraid the Baron and His Majesty the King rode out early this morning and will not return until following the Baron's wedding."

"What? Out riding now? On the morning of his wedding?" Nurse Joan sounded bitterly disappointed.

The steward took a tiny step away from the raging woman before explaining, "They have undertaken a gentleman's hunt in hopes of catching the white stag and incurring good fortune on the Baron's marriage."

As the steward's words sunk in, a huge wave a of relief filled me with miraculous energy. "You mean Sophia's not … the wedding hasn't … Where is Sophia now?"

"Silence!" Nurse Joan hissed. "Mistress Sophia is being dressed for her wedding, but that is no concern of yours."

I smiled right back at Nurse Joan. She could shout at me all she liked. All that mattered was that it wasn't too late! So much relief poured over me, like warm water thawing ice. I could have laughed or cried, or both.

The corners of Nurse Joan's tight mouth turned down in serious displeasure. I thought she might punch the steward.

He must've thought he was in danger too, because he very quickly piped up, "The Baron cannot receive you; however, Her Majesty the Queen is taking audience this morning until such time as she must depart to escort her niece to her wedding. She will see you about this *urgent* matter."

Nurse Joan's puckered mouth turned upward again as

the steward pushed open the double doors and led us into a very large, square room with tall, decorated ceilings and a red carpet running down the middle of the floor to a dais. On the dais were two thrones, and in the smaller one sat the Queen in a gold and burgundy brocade gown, dripping in pearls. Her red hair was piled high like a hive on top of her head. But what I noticed most was her face — powdered and unsmiling though it was, she had a kindly, motherly face with clever eyes that reminded me a little of Sophia. That gave me hope.

The steward led us right down to the carpet just in front of the dais, then stopped and bowed low. The man holding my arm copied, forcing me to bend over at the same time.

"What is this, Walter?" the Queen asked in her Danish accent.

"Your Majesty, this woman wishes to bring an urgent matter of treason before you."

"Oh? And is this delicate creature the traitor?" Her ruby lips pressed together as she looked at me, as if she were trying not to smile. I could see she thought Nurse Joan's charge of treason against me, skinny little girl, was a joke.

"Your Majesty," — Nurse Joan croaked. She sounded much less confident before the grandeur of the Queen and her watching courtiers — "I do suspect … nay, *know* beyond a doubt that this girl has some evil power and has applied it in the murder of my Master and the affliction of my Mistress."

The Queen was unmoved except for one raised

eyebrow. "Is that so? You suppose this little kitchen maid to be a witch? On what grounds, madam?"

"Why, your Highness ..." Nurse Joan looked around as if hoping for someone to volunteer an answer. "She ... she speaks and behaves so strangely. And her hair is ..." she checked herself just in time.

"What about her hair?" The Queen sounded indignant.

"I was going to say *short*. Her hair is too short, Majesty."

"Of course." The Queen was obviously not convinced. "Carry on."

"It was only after she mysteriously arrived at this house that all the ill fell upon it. And what's more, yesterday she disappeared during her duties and I caught her just last night sneaking about the household corridors. No doubt she was putting hexes on the family."

I watched the Queen's face throughout Nurse Joan's absurd accusations. Her expression never changed; she didn't appear to believe any of it. But I couldn't be sure. As superstitious as King James was, his wife might be of a similar paranoid way of thinking. And if she was, I might easily wind up in the jail cell beside Digby and Bessy within minutes. Or worse ...

When Nurse Joan finished, the Queen scrutinised me from her throne, then asked, "What have you to say for yourself against these accusations, little wench? Do you deny them?"

I decided right then to risk everything. I had no choice; there were no other tricks up my sleeve. I cleared my throat and spoke up as confidently as I imagined Sophia would do in my place. "Your Majesty, before the Baron sent me to the kitchens, I was your niece Sophia's personal companion and closest friend. I was at the banquet the night the Earl was murdered, and I know how it happened. It wasn't Frederick. It was the Baron himself."

The Queen's expression shifted for the first time at that. Her mouth opened in a gasp, but I pushed on. "The reason I was sneaking around the house was to gather the evidence to prove the truth to the King before it's too late and innocent people die … not to mention Sophia's life will be ruined because she'll be married to the man who murdered her guardian and her brother." I stopped, expecting the Queen to say something, but she only looked at me with interest, waiting to hear more. "Your Majesty, please. If you could just speak to the King and ask him to stop the wedding and the executions until he has seen this evidence …"

"What you tell me is … dare I say … what I've suspected. My nephew Frederick could not be the murderer. He had nothing to gain from it, while the Baron had many reasons to remove his brother and his heir."

I couldn't believe it. This was better than I could've hoped for! "So you will speak to the King?"

The sad look on the Queen's face deflated my happiness. "I have no influence over my husband in this matter," she said bitterly. "You must understand, I have already tried to defend Frederick's innocence and begged the King to look more carefully into the matter. But Frederick is my sister's son, which the King believes has made me a blind judge, unable to accept the boy's true nature."

"But it's the King who's a blind judge to the Baron's true nature!" I blurted. There was a gasp from every servant and courtier in the room, but I couldn't care less. He wasn't *my* king anyhow. I pressed forward. "There's so much evidence of the truth, Your Majesty. If the King would only listen …"

"You have my sympathy, my dear. But the Baron speaks out with a strong voice against witchcraft and treason, the two subjects my husband finds most odious. The King believes he has found a close ally in the Baron. But I wonder, what manner of evidence is this of which you speak?"

I threw back my cloak and slung my backpack around in what felt like one very dramatic movement. "Irrefutable evidence," I answered. The Queen listened carefully while I recounted every step of my journey to discovering Master Van Hoebeek as the true murderer, and then his true identity as the Baron in disguise. And as I explained, I produced my evidence, one piece at a time. "*This* is the disguise he wore when he stood before the King and accused Frederick, the very night before Master Van Hoebeek supposedly rushed off to Holland and the Baron *just happened* to turn up the next day."

The Queen's face grew more and more horrified, just as I'd hoped. It egged me on to the next piece of evidence. "I'm not positive, but I think this bottle is the very poison the Baron dropped into the Earl's goblet that night, and I have it on good grounds that he's been poisoning the Countess as well, keeping her alive just long enough so that her death doesn't look too suspicious."

The Queen looked aghast. "Can this be true?"

"Ask Nurse Joan for the medicinal draught she's been

giving the Countess under the Baron's orders. I'm sure you'll find it's poison."

She turned sharply towards Nurse Joan with raised eyebrows. "Nurse Joan, the draught, if you please. I will have my own apothecaries inspect it."

Nurse Joan had gone ghostly white, her hawk eyes now more like bug eyes and full of bewilderment. "Your Majesty, I never had the slightest notion of it being poison, I ... I swear it by the Almighty."

I stepped forward. "She's telling the truth, Your Majesty. I don't believe Nurse Joan ever meant to hurt her Mistress. She was only following bad orders."

The wiry old housemaid looked as though someone had slapped her. She lowered her eyes to the floor, and I could see her jaw clenching as she backed slowly against the wall.

"We shall see," the Queen answered. "Now, have you anything else in that most unusual satchel?"

I pulled out the stack of letters and offered them to the steward who in turn delivered them into the Queen's hand. "They're the Baron's letters. I found them with the other items, but I can't quite make out the handwriting."

In a very business-like manner, the Queen untied the red ribbon and unfolded the first letter. As she read, her eyes widened and darted faster and faster over the page. The strings of pearls on her chest rose and fell with her quickening breath. "Bring me the bottle at once." She held out her open hand while the steward took the bottle from me and delivered it to the Queen. She uncorked it, closed her eyes and held it to her nose. Although the Queen's face was powdered white, I almost fancied she became a shade whiter. "'Tis Inheritance Powder," she muttered as if she'd just seen a ghost. She handed the bottle back to the steward and returned her face to its usual composed, statue-like expression. "My dear, do you have any idea what this is?" She waved the letter.

"It looks like some sort of recipe?" I asked, afraid of sounding childish.

"Not just any recipe. It is the recipe for a witch's potion concocted especially for the purpose of killing off one's relatives in order to claim their inheritance for one's self. What is more, it is addressed to the Baron and signed by what appears to be a most ... particular friend of his, Mistress Liddy Thompson."

I didn't know what to say. The Queen promptly folded the letter up and tucked the whole lot into a fold in her gown. "Walter, I would speak with ... what is your name, child?"

I cleared my throat. "Watson, Your Majesty. Katherine Watson."

She bowed her head. "I would speak with Mistress Katherine Watson alone. Clear the hall, if you please."

Walter made the announcement. It was followed by a general murmur, a rustle of skirts, then finally, as Walter pushed the doors shut with only himself, the Queen and me inside, silence.

"Come closer, my dear. Yes, sit here on the stair, just beside me."

I did as I was told, feeling suddenly conscious of being in the presence of a Queen while smelling of a meat locker; and I didn't even want to know what state my hair was in.

The Queen leaned forward in her chair, and I knew

from the intense look in her eyes, she was about to say something important. She spoke in a low, voice, enunciating each word to be sure I understood. "Katherine, I believe all that you have just revealed to me. And I believe there is yet time to persuade the King before it is too late. But it will be a delicate matter. Can I count upon you?"

I nodded wholeheartedly. "Yes, Your Majesty. What shall I do?"

"In a mere hour's time, I will escort Sophia to the church in my carriage. The King and the Baron will be awaiting us, and the wedding will begin promptly at midday. That is the time to reveal the Baron's schemes, when he is away from home and cornered between this evidence and God's altar. Be certain the King sees *all* that you have shown me. Especially these." She handed me back the letters. "But you must not tell anyone of this conversation. If the King knew that I advised you in any way, he may presume that I have contrived the whole thing and not give ear to what you have to say. Do you understand?"

"Yes." I nodded.

"It is a dangerous undertaking, Katherine. I am sorry to ask it of you. Are you prepared?"

"It's not nearly as bad as the risk of *not* doing it," I replied.

The Queen smiled her first truly warm smile. "You are courageous of heart, my child. But I do wish there were someone who might stand beside you."

"But there is. Oh, Your Majesty, I almost forgot to tell you! It's not Frederick in the jail."

She looked utterly bewildered, but once I'd explained

how the two boys had swapped places and Frederick was safely hidden with Tom, the Queen put her hand over her heart and looked as though she might cry for joy. "Then he is safe. Now, you must go to them at once! We have not a minute to lose. God be with you, Katherine Watson, until we meet again." She held out her hand to me. I wasn't quite sure what to do with it, so I took it and gave it a gentle shake. She pressed her red lips together again like she was holding in a laugh. I guessed I was probably meant to kiss her hand instead of shaking it. But I didn't have the chance to correct my mistake. The Queen called to Walter and asked him to personally escort me to the gatehouse and see that nobody delayed my journey. He bowed and waited for me to walk out first.

"Thank you, Your Majesty. God bless you!" I said, and nearly skipped my way down the red carpet with poor Walter trying to keep in pace with me. But my heart was too full of the hope of a second chance to slow down. The rescue mission was back on!

RIDE TO THE RESCUE

"Tom, Frederick! I've got it! I've got the evidence! There's STILL TIME!" I skidded into the forest glade and stopped in front of the shepherd's wagon. I had run so fast, my heart felt like it might explode.

Vagabond whinnied a greeting, but no other response came. Perhaps Tom and Frederick were keeping cover in the wagon. My hand was on the door, ready to slide it back, when it opened and Frederick stuck out his dishevelled head. My eyes went straight away to the sword hanging at his waist. His hand rested on its hilt.

"Good God, Katie! We were certain you were captured."

"I was," I panted. "Nurse Joan locked me in the meat cellar all night, but then I spoke to the Queen, and she believes us … about everything!"

"The Queen believes us?" He looked confused, as though he hadn't quite heard me right. "How …"

"I showed her the evidence. That was all it took, and she thinks when the King sees it, he'll believe it too. But

Frederick, there's no time to explain the rest now. Where's Tom?"

"When you didn't return, he disguised himself again and went back to the Manor. He hoped Jack Hornsby would help him find out what had become of you."

"Oh no …" I groaned. "There's no time! Frederick, the Baron lied to Sophia. He doesn't mean to release the prisoners after the wedding at all. I head two guards talking. Digby and Bessy are going to be hanged as soon as the church bells toll after the wedding."

Frederick pushed past me and leapt down the step ladder, drawing his sword like he was in the middle of a battle. "No longer will I hide like a craven while a good man dies in my place. I am Lord of this house, and I shall not sit idly by while such a crime is committed." He looked fearsome, but all the fight quickly deflated out of him. He looked around as if lost, his sword hanging limp. "But Sophia. I must save Sophia, though saving her may cost the lives of Digby and Bessy. What am I to do?"

I jumped down from the step ladder and marched over to him. "I'll go and rescue Sophia. You find Tom." He looked as though he wanted to object, but he let me finish. "Hopefully the two of you plus Jack and anyone else who will help can hold off the execution until the King returns. Your servants hate the Baron. I've heard them complaining about him in the kitchens. They'll listen to you!"

Frederick's chest rose up proudly once again. "You're right. It's time I took my place as their Earl. But Katie, it's barely twenty minutes to midday now. How will you stop the wedding in time?"

I gritted my teeth and looked frantically around for an

answer. It came to me from behind, in the form of a snort. "I'll ride."

He looked at me like I was loony. "What, Vagabond? *Nobody's* been able to mount that horse. He's thrown off the entire King's guard. Katie, you cannot ..."

I didn't wait for him to finish. I marched over to the hitching post and untied Vagabond's tether. I nestled against his muscular shoulder and reached my hand up to stroke his neck. "I need you, Vagabond. Please," I whispered. He lowered his head as if truly listening. "Let's do this together." I stepped back and took one enormous breath. "Will you help me up?" I asked Frederick.

"Are you sure, Katie? He could kill you."

"He won't kill me." I hoped I was right. "And yes, I'm sure."

Frederick shook his head, but he came. He cupped his hands together and held them out. I gave Vagabond one last look in the eye and nodded. Breathing deeply, steadily, I raised one trembling hand up and got a handful of his mane, stepped my foot into Frederick's cupped hands and pushed off, swinging my leg over the horse and coming to sit squarely on his broad back. For an uncertain moment, Vagabond pranced backward and forward as if he didn't know what to make of things. I knew just how he felt. I leant over and stroked his neck. "It's ok, Vagabond. We've got this." I looked at Frederick and nodded. "Good luck."

Frederick looked tense as he backed away. I'm sure he expected the horse to rear up and send me flying to my death at any moment. I filled my fists with Vagabond's thick mane, hugged tightly to his sides with my calves and urged him forward.

Like a bolt of electricity had zapped him into action, Vagabond gave a heroic whinny and shot off. Up the hill, careening through trees, leaping over fallen logs in our path. Soon we were out into the open meadows with a mist stinging our faces and a stormy wind whipping my hair back.

Brum drum, Brum drum, Brum drum. Vagabond's hooves beat our coming, like a mighty war drum. Though we might have been riding to our doom, my heart swelled up and burst into a smile across my wind-blown face. *This was joy.*

Vagabond felt it too, I knew he did. I hardly needed to steer him. He knew what I was thinking, just as Gypsy used to do. Soon we were flying through the park gates and up the lane to the parish church where already the bell was tolling the arrival of the Queen and Sophia. Carriages filled the narrow, pebbly street outside the church, but Vagabond manoeuvred around them like a champion dressage horse. We skidded to a halt in the churchyard in a cloud of dirt and gravel. I hoisted myself off his back and landed with a dusty thud on the gravel. I didn't bother to tether Vagabond; I was sure when I came out of that church, for better or for worse, he would be there waiting for me.

An amazing thing happened to me on that glorious ride. All my hunger, my exhaustion, all my fear had been blown away with the wind. I felt the fierceness I'd seen in Frederick's eyes when he'd brandished that sword. I was as ready as I'd ever be to face the enemy.

There was only one thing stopping me. The doors were locked. I bashed my body against them, but they didn't budge. I banged on them with my fist, but nobody answered. My banging was drowned out by the thunder of a booming organ. *This is stupid*, I thought, kicking the gravel. *I did not come all the way from the twenty-first century to let a door stand in my way.*

A crazy idea dropped into my head. I led Vagabond over to a tombstone and climbed up it to mount him, then rode him out a way into the churchyard. "Alright, Vagabond. I need you to harness all that anger you've been using to smash pigeons and take it out on those doors. Ready?" He whinnied, which was a good enough answer for me.

"Ya!" I yelled, kicking his sides with a force that sent him bolting forward with a vengeance towards the doors. Right when it looked like we would smash into them, he reared up on his back legs and pummelled them with his two, boulder-sized front hooves. We smashed right through them and didn't stop until Vagabond had cantered right down the aisle to the middle of the church.

The organ played a sour chord. Screams and shouts rent the perfumed air. The King stood up from his golden throne on the dais. His eyes were wild with what could only be terror. He pointed his finger and bellowed, "God save me! 'Tis that demon horse and the devil's child herself come to torment me!"

"No, Your Majesty," I called out, pulling back on Vagabond's mane to bring him to standing. "The only devil here is that man." I pointed my finger at the Baron where he stood in front of the bride and groom's chairs. At his side, Sophia beamed. "*He* is the traitor," I shouted loud and clear.

The room fell completely silent. All eyes zeroed in on the King. The King looked at the Baron, then at me on the horse. The Queen caught my eye and nodded a "go on" sort of nod.

"I have evidence, Your Majesty. And witnesses."

"What is this? Who are you? What is this evidence? Who are these witnesses?" The King sounded more desperate with every question.

"I am a witness." Sophia stepped forward. She looked so queenly in her enormous golden skirts that the Baron appeared small and puny, even with all his ruffles and lace. "Please Your Majesties to hear what she has to say. This is Katherine Watson, my most intimate friend, and I will speak for her truthfulness."

"As will I!" A shock wave went through the pews as everyone turned to see Frederick standing in the doorway with Tom Tippery, Jack Hornsby and a dozen armed men at his back. They looked fierce, panting and sweating and with the fire of justice in their eyes.

The Baron stepped forward, his glowing charcoal eyes full of bewilderment. "It can't be. Why aren't you locked away, getting fitted for your noose? You should be hanging by the time my wedding is finished!"

"You monster!" Sophia shouted and stormed off the dais to stand beside her brother. "You never arrested Frederick, because he wasn't even there the night of the banquet when *you* murdered the Earl. You arrested a stable hand."

The Baron went scarlet. "How dare you accuse me! You forget that *I* was not present when the Earl was murdered," he growled, baring his teeth like a cornered tiger.

"You know that's a lie, and we can prove it!" I dropped to the ground and ran up the steps onto the dais. Yanking the woollen beard from my backpack, I waved it in the air for all to see. "Here is your Master Van Hoebeek, Your Majesty. Put him in his black sheep beard and you'll see for yourself."

At first, no one moved. Then in a split second, the Baron made a dart for the side door, and the King shouted, "Seize that man!"

Two guardsmen dragged the Baron to the middle of the dais, before the King and in full view of every courtier in the place. His nostrils flared with anger. "This is madness, Your Majesty. Surely you'll not be taken in by children and riff-raff."

"Madness or not, Baron, I will see you wear that beard."

I stepped forward, giving the beard along with the hat and wig to the guards. One of them fitted them onto the Baron then stepped back for the King to see.

When he had taken a good look, he staggered backwards a step or two. "It looks the same as the man that did stand before me with talk of plots and witchcraft. But can it truly be?"

"I have more evidence, Your Majesty." I gave the guardsman the bottle and the letters. "These were taken from the Baron's trunk in a room where he's been hiding his secrets at Otterly Manor, along with Bessy Tippery who, by the way, only confessed because *he* threatened her."

The King's skittish eyes flitted over the first letter. He held out his hand for the bottle, sniffed it, turned away. When he turned back, he looked frightful, every bit the angry Scotsman. His moustache twitched and his eyes bulged. When he spoke, his voice was more thunderous than the organ pipes. He raised his finger to the Baron. "I have had my fill of murderous plots. First that papish rogue Guy Fawkes. Now you?" His voice rose to a shout. "Is none of my kingdom's nobility safe from plotters?" He turned away and brandished his hand in the air. "Guards! Arrest the Baron. Transport him immediately to the Tower to await sentence."

"Majesty, 'tis trickery!" The Baron screeched as the guards bound up his hands with ropes. "These *fiends* blind you with witchcraft!"

"Silence! I will not listen to warnings of trickery from a master of deception."

The Baron shouted and struggled against the guards all the way down the aisle. He only stopped to curse and swear vengeance at the group of us standing around the horse in the middle of the church. Chances are, he never stopped screaming and cursing all the way to the Tower.

28

THE EARL'S COURT

$\mathcal{W}$hat had begun as the most miserable day of my nearly twelve years ended as one of the happiest. Once the Baron was good and out of the way, the King publicly cleared Frederick of all accusations, then and there at the front of the church.

Then, of course, Frederick insisted we return to the Manor where Digby and Bessy still sat in prison cells. Apparently, most of the Otterly Manor household servants had sided with Frederick when he'd turned up, and that was enough to keep the King's guardsmen from doing anything rash. But they'd refused to set the prisoners free without the King's orders.

We led the procession of courtiers in their carriages up the lane and through the park to Otterly Manor. I rode Vagabond alongside Sophia who rode in the Queen's carriage.

"Just wait until Digby and Jack see you riding that horse as if he's a show pony!" Sophia called out the window. She was dressed like a little queen, but she giggled as merrily as a child at Christmas. I could see she was enormously relieved by the way she couldn't stop beaming at everybody, but especially at Frederick and me.

THE GUARDS RELEASED Digby and Bessy immediately once the King gave the command. Digby clasped Frederick's hand and hugged Sophia and me. Bessy and Tom wept in each other's arms. But it soon became clear that the two prisoners hadn't been quite as miserable in their cells as we'd all feared. The two of them kept close together and kept giving each other dreamy glances. I'd seen Charlie make the same, disgusting faces at his high-school sweetheart.

We knew something was definitely up when King James not only pardoned Digby for his crime of dressing in courtier's clothing (Frederick explained that Digby acted on his orders), but offered to make him a steward at the palace for showing such loyalty to his lord.

"I need more men in my service like you whom I can trust with my life," the King said. "Pack up your effects and you may join us when we return to Court on the morrow."

Digby gaped like a fish. Then he took one look at Bessy and knelt before the King. "Your Majesty does me the greatest honour. But, if it please Your Highness, I think I've had my fill of Court life. Prison and near death changes a man. Makes him think about what he really wants in life." His eyes darted over to Bessy then returned to the King. "I'd prefer to go back to work in the stables, if I may, Your Highness. Earn an honest wage … enough to provide one day for a wife and children." He shot Bessy another sheepish glance. Her cheeks went pink.

The King hadn't missed the look between them. "With my blessing." He leant down as if confiding in Digby, but spoke loud enough for us all to hear. "But I believe 'tis not my permission, but rather the maid's father's you have need of."

Digby blushed then and grinned like a jester. He got up off his knees and went to Tom who'd been watching the whole comical episode. "Master Tippery, I haven't any fineries to offer her, but I promise to treat Bess just like the lady she is."

Tom took his daughter's hand and joined it to Digby's. "If your love could blossom in a prison cell, I have no doubt it will flourish ever after." Bessy kissed her father's cheek while Frederick and Jack slapped Digby hard on the back.

Everyone was in a holiday mood and ready to celebrate. It seemed a pity to waste the seven-course wedding feast the Baron had ordered, especially when Mary Haye's and her crew of kitchen hands had laboured day and night to prepare it. So Frederick — *Earl* Frederick that is — declared an Exoneration Feast, and invited the entire household, servants and all, to join in!

Sophia and I twirled each other around when Frederick announced there would be music and dancing, though at that point, I was more excited about the food. I still hadn't eaten since the day before. Sophia noticed how pale I was and ordered soup, bread and cheese to be brought to me in the bedchamber while we discussed the important business of what to wear to the feast.

It felt heavenly to be back in the red bedchamber again. Everything was back to normal. Sophia and I chattered away and laughed at any and every little thing. Britannia stretched out in front of the hearth on the Turkish rug. It seemed as if the Baron and the past two horrific days was no more than a bad dream fading from memory.

While I gobbled down my soup, a maid came in to deliver the good news that the Countess was improving since the Queen stopped her "medicine". She would see us both in the morning. She'd heard the whole story about the Baron and wanted to thank the little maid who had done so much for her household.

"How I do hope Nurse Joan is waiting on the Countess in the morning," Sophia said. "She deserves all the humble pie she gets."

I sighed. "I think Nurse Joan would be happy never to lay eyes on my devil-kissed hair ever again." We laughed till I was choking on soup.

Tatty and Elinor were in a chirpy mood when they came to help us dress, possibly because the new Earl had invited them to the feast as well. They removed Sophia's wedding dress, which weighed as much as a full-grown rhinoceros. She exchanged it for a simple, pale blue silk one. I traded my kitchen maid uniform for my old yellow velvet gown, and we were ready.

"I'll see you on the dance floor!" I said when we'd got to the bottom of the Great Staircase.

"Katie, you jest! Of course you are to sit at High Table with the rest of us. This is an Exoneration Feast. Nobody would have been exonerated today if it weren't for you." She took my hand. "*You* are the guest of honour."

That evening was perfection. All of my fondest acquaintances from Otterly Manor were there — Digby with Bessy, Jack Hornsby, Tom — all mixed in among the courtiers and having a whale of a time. We ate the Baron's choice dishes, toasted the new Earl, and danced till the sun went down and the firelight cast its dreamy spell.

But something pestered at the back of my mind all evening, even as I danced and ate and laughed. The images I'd conjured the night before of my family kept pushing into my mind's eye, and I kept pushing them back again. Only when I lay in bed with Sophia breathing peacefully beside me, did the feeling crash over me like an ocean breaker. There was no mistaking that deep, hollow ache. I was homesick.

Now I'd done the thing I thought I'd come to do, what next? I loved Sophia like a sister, and Frederick and Digby had become almost like brothers to me. But nothing could replace my own life, my family. I closed my eyes and let the pictures come into full focus. When I woke, my heart felt as heavy as a pail full of water.

29

GOODBYES

*T*he morning sun veiled the forests and meadows of Otterly Park in silver gossamer when the household lined up outside the gatehouse to send off the Royal Court.

One by one, the carriages paraded up the hill to carry away their lords and ladies to the next great house on the royal tour. Frederick did his duty as host like a pro, graciously thanking each and every member of the Court by name and offering his future hospitality. When at last the royal carriage topped the hill, its wheel spokes glistening gold, the King and Queen themselves offered their goodbyes.

When the King came to me, he said a civil farewell, and I curtseyed back. But the Queen smiled with real warmth and offered me her hand. This time I was prepared, but before I could bend over to kiss it, she gave mine a gentle shake. Her eyes twinkled. "I do not know the family Watson, but I hope you will give your parents my regard and tell them the Queen says their daughter does them great credit."

"Thank you, Your Majesty," I managed to peep as I curtseyed low.

As we watched the royal carriage disappear behind the park's bracken curtains, Sophia linked her arm through mine, and we meandered back under the gatehouse archway. "The Queen is right, you know. You do your family great credit. And a family with so noble a daughter deserve to have her with them again."

"Then what about you?" I argued, afraid that admitting my homesickness might let loose the knot forming in my throat. "You're the one who's truly noble. I don't think I'd have married the Baron for anything! Doesn't your family deserve to have you back as well?"

Sophia smiled. "I have family here." She gave Frederick, walking alongside the steward, a look full of pride and admiration. But concern filled her face when she turned back to me. "Katie, tell me. Something weighs on your mind. You have brought happiness to all of us at Otterly Manor. I wish so much I could help you find your own."

We sat down on a bench in the grassy courtyard. The knot in my throat kept getting tighter. "Oh Sophia, I know I have to make the most of my circumstances, and you're all like family to me, but ..." One insistent tear squeezed its way out and fell into my lap.

"But Katie, you *have* made the most of the very worst of circumstances. And now you wish for home. That is not ingratitude. It is only natural in all creatures blessed with a heart to long for home."

"I'm not sure that ... that there *is* a way back home." I

wiped my eyes as another tear swelled up, ready to take the last one's place. "I spoke to Tom, but he doesn't exactly seem to know how the magic worked, or how to make it work again. It all comes down to these strange paints he bought off some woman, and heart's desires and … oh I don't know."

Sophia offered me her handkerchief and waited for me to blow my nose before she spoke. "I'm not sure there's a way either, Katie. But you mustn't give up hope. I spoke to Tom last night too." Still wiping my nose, I gave her a questioning side look. "Yes. Last night while you were dancing with Frederick. He has an idea, and I believe it is worth a try."

WE TOOK our time walking to Tom's wagon, enjoying the sun puddles beneath the trees, the smell of sweet grass, the hilarious sight of Tannia stalking up behind unsuspecting deer only to lunge out of the bracken and send them springing far and wide. Most of all, we enjoyed being two friends out on a summer's walk with a dog and not a single worry of nurses, maids or tutors calling after us to come inside at once and behave like little grown-ups.

We found Tom in his usual spot, concentrating over his easel before a smouldering fire that sent up those familiar wisps of smoke.

Tom spared a quick glance in our direction, then returned to the painting. "To what do I owe the honour of a visit from two such fine ladies?"

I stopped to cradle Vagabond's nose before plopping

down beside the fire in a not-so-lady-like manner. "We've just come for a visit. What are you painting now?"

"Oh it's just a little experiment really. In fact, I'd value your advice."

"*My* advice? Sophia's the better artist. You should see her birds!"

Sophia shook her yellow head modestly and gracefully sat on the stump beside me. "You know, Tom, Frederick would gladly give you quarters in the Manor. Now the Court has gone, there are plenty of rooms."

"The Earl is exceedingly generous," Tom answered. "I hear he has also offered Digby and Bessy a cottage on the grounds once they are wed. But I confess, I have grown too fond of the tranquillity in this glade." He nodded his head towards Vagabond. "He seems content here away from the crowds as well."

"Then you need never move your wagon from this spot," Sophia said.

"What will you do now?" I asked. "With Bessy settled at Otterly Manor, surely you won't wish to travel for work any longer."

Placing his paintbrush down, Tom took off his cloth cap and turned it in his hands. "My wrongs have been mercifully righted. My daughter is provided for. What more could a man wish for than that?"

"But you deserve to be a true master painter," I insisted. "I've never seen nicer paintings than yours."

Tom smiled but kept his eyes down. "It is kind of you to say so. Coincidentally, the Queen expressed some interest in my work and requested a piece for her salon. Who knows what may come of it."

"Is that what you're working on now?" I pried. "The piece you want advice on? Can we have a look?" I squeezed past Sophia to walk around Tom and have a look over his shoulder. "Is that … me?"

I looked up and caught Sophia smiling.

"This piece is for something far more important than the Queen's salon," Tom said, adding a stroke of red to my portrait's hair. Only then did I notice he was using paints from the wooden box. The swirling colours took life on the canvas. The strands of my hair almost seemed to be waving in a soft breeze.

"This is Tom's idea," Sophia explained. "A family portrait. *Your* family portrait."

"And now you see why I rely on your advice," Tom added. "For I have never seen your family."

"Wait," I said, trying to get a grip one what was happening. "You think that if you, with my help, paint my family all together, the painting will take me home when I look at it?"

Tom shrugged apologetically. "I cannot promise it will work, but it was the best I could come up with."

"Try, Katie," Sophia urged.

I took a deep breath. "Alright. I'll do my best. What shall I do?"

"Just describe them, one by one, as best you can."

So for the next hour, I sat on the log with my eyes squeezed tightly shut, remembering all the mental portraits I'd painted of my family over and over again in the last day and a half. There was Dad with his messy auburn hair and stubbly chin; Mum, tall with strawberry hair like mine and dimples like Nan's; then Charlie with his signature sideways grin. I described every detail I could think of while Sophia picked up a lute propped against the wagon and strummed quietly. Meanwhile, Tom dashed stroke after stroke of paint onto his canvas.

At last I ran out of things to describe. Tom added a few finishing touches and sat back to examine. "I'd ask you to tell me what you think, but there's a risk you won't get the chance to answer once you look."

I gulped. On the one hand, the idea of looking at that canvas and nothing happening was too terrible to imagine. But on the other hand, the idea of being whisked back to the twenty-first century and leaving behind all the friends I'd come to love forever …

I turned around slowly, afraid to look at Sophia. She had stopped strumming and her eyes were brimming with tears. Still she smiled. "You've saved my life and many others besides. Now your life is waiting, Katie."

"It may not work, you know," I said through my own tears and ran to throw my arms around her. We stood there hugging and crying.

Tannia's nuzzle pressed against my side and she whimpered. "Here, Tannia." Sophia released me to remove my bag and take from it the ball sling and spare tennis ball. I knelt and held it out in my arms as if offering a sword to a knight. "This is for you. I'm leaving it in Sophia's care." I handed it over to Sophia, and we both laughed through our tears. There was a stamp and whinny from behind. I wiped my eyes. Vagabond must've sensed it was goodbye. He pranced and reared his head in agitation.

Sophia let me go to him. I put my arms around his colossal head and leaned my head against his strong, smooth neck. "Thank you," I whispered. "You have a good life now. And no more pigeon smashing." I kissed his nose and turned away quickly.

The tears poured out in an unstoppable stream now so that Tom's face in front of me looked like an impressionist painting. But I could see his eyes were smiling. He put a handkerchief into my hand. "Best dry those eyes. You'll need them clear if it is to work."

I dried up the tears, taking deep, slow breaths to try and stop more from welling up.

"Better?"

Now the twinkle in Tom's eye was perfectly clear. I nodded, then saw that he held his closed hand out to me. "What's this?" I asked.

He gently took my hand and placed a small, smooth object into it. "A memory."

In my hand was a golden chain and locket. I opened it up and had to hold my breath to keep the tears from starting all over again. On one side of the locket was a miniature portrait of two girls standing side-by-side, one with golden hair, the other with strawberry blonde. In the other half, there was a tiny portrait of a big, black horse.

I felt Tom watching, waiting for some response, but I couldn't speak a word. I flung my arms around his neck instead. He gently patted my head with his rough hand. "Come," he whispered. "'Tis time."

I took hold of Sophia's hand and clasped it tightly. Together we walked around the easel. I shut my eyes for one last breath, then …

I was looking at my family's faces. There they all were, gathered around me and as lifelike as if it had been a photograph. I felt the urge to touch them, to see if they felt as real as they looked. I reached out my hand to touch the canvas, and I fell. Through browns and greens of the forest, through golden light, the colours swirled and danced all around me like the paints in Tom's box. And then the world stopped and stood still.

When I opened my eyes — but when had I closed them? — I sat gripping my knees in a pool of light. I was in the secret chamber. There was the rusty old chest, just as before. And there on the wall in front of me was Tom's painting. For just a moment, I wondered if I'd hit my head and imagined the whole thing up. But as I was about to reach up and feel my forehead for bumps, I realised I was clutching something smooth and round in my palm. It was a gold locket.

*P*op rolled down the car window at the ticket kiosk and handed the girl in the uniform his membership card. She digitally scanned it and handed it back. "Enjoy your visit to Otterly Manor," she said flashing a metallic smile from her braces. The gates opened automatically, and we drove into the park.

"You know, Katie," Pop said to me in the rear-view mirror, "Your Nan and I hoped you'd enjoy this place, but we worried it might be a tad ... well, boring for you. We're so pleased you liked it well enough to want to bring your parents."

"I know," Mum chimed in. "Who knew our Katie was such a keen historian!"

"Otterly Manor," Dad repeated to himself like he was trying to recall something. "That's it! I'd almost forgotten! You won't believe what a small world it is, but I actually read something about a murder mystery that took place in this house at a museum in Edinburgh. I'm sorry you weren't with us, Katie. I know how much you would've enjoyed it."

"It's alright. A girl can't expect to go on an adventure every summer," I answered, watching the park go by out my window. "But what was it you read about Otterly Manor, Dad?"

"Oh right. Well apparently, there was a great mystery surrounding the Earl's death back in Tudor Stuart times."

"Is that so?" Pop asked, pulling into a space in the gravel car park.

"It turned out he was murdered by his own brother in disguise as a painter. And what's more, it was a young serving girl who solved the mystery. Now there's some interesting history for you, Katie. Just like something out of Sherlock Holmes."

"Yup," I said, jumping out of the car and taking stock of the familiar rolling, bracken-covered hills.

Oscar squirmed at Pop's heels while he rummaged around the boot of the car for something. "Now where did I put that ball sling? I must be going senile." Pop scratched his bald patch. "Sorry, Oscar. Just walkies today."

I bit my lip and took off towards the field on the stable-side of the house with Oscar.

After a walk around the park, we stopped for a spot of tea and cake in the old prison, now converted into the café. *Frederick would be pleased with this change at least,* I thought, filling my nostrils with the scrumptious aroma of fresh scones.

Mum and I made a quick visit to the café loos before taking on the house proper. I stopped outside the men's loo and gaped in disbelief at the door. The Baron's portrait hung from it, but instead of the ribbon across the top inscribed *Second Earl of Dorset,* there was only a wooden plaque with the world "Gents" printed on it.

"The ladies' is this side, Katherine," Mum said when she realised I had fallen back.

"Oh, right," I answered, and waited till she'd turned around to indulge in a quick heel click.

Finally we entered the house, starting the self-guided tour at the Great Hall which was once again faded and smelled of old things. But my heart leapt all the same remembering the sensation of dancing by firelight to the sweet music wafting down from the musician's box.

"Would you like a children's guide, ducky?" The old man held it out to me in his shaky hand. "There's a prize if you find all the objects."

I took it and found myself naturally curtseying. "Thank you," I said, quickly pretending to bend down to tie my shoe.

As we walked along, our footsteps echoing in the life-less, empty room, I explained to Mum and Dad about the High Table and the servant's tables. "The most important people would have sat up there, where the portrait of the Second Earl is hung." The painting was very like Frederick, though a slightly older, even more dashing version of him. "Of course, the family only ate in here on special occasions, banquets and feasts and the like. Then there'd be live music and theatrical performances … Did you know Shakespeare's company performed Macbeth here for King James?"

"My, Katie. You certainly have learned a lot!" Nan

exclaimed. "Next time I must pick up one of those children's guides."

In the Billiard Gallery, Nan and Pop drew Mum and Dad over to the china cabinet. I was happy to break away on my own and have a moment just to take in the place. Naturally, my feet took me down to the other end of the long gallery where the secret chamber was hidden. An elderly couple occupied the corner with the Green Man. I waited my turn, pretending to look out the windows at the park.

"Pardon me," the elderly man waved to the stocky volunteer, and she eagerly waddled over. "We were wondering, can you tell us the meaning of this peculiar object the girl's holding in this portrait?" Peeking over my shoulder, I saw they were standing right in front of a portrait of Sophia! Britannia sat upright by her side with Sophia's hand resting on her head. Cradled in her other arm, was the ball sling.

A laugh escaped me before I could stop it which made the volunteer turn and glare before launching into her smug explanation. "Yes, of course. That is a ... erm .... Well obviously it's some sort of ... it's a riding whip. Yes, you see young ladies were expected to be good at riding horseback. By including the whip, the artist has drawn our attention to this young lady's accomplishments and suitability for marriage."

"How very interesting," the elderly man commented.

I curled my lips inward to keep from laughing again and didn't dare step away from the window until the couple, and the volunteer, had moved on. Only then could I visit with my dear friend in peace. Though it didn't do her justice, it was a beautiful portrait. No longer did Sophia wear a sad expression. She smiled. I smiled back at her and noticed a signature on the bottom of the painting: *Master Thomas Tippery*.

"Well done, Tom," I whispered as if somehow he could hear me.

BACK IN THE CAR, I leaned my head against the window and listened to my family chat about ordinary old stuff. I sighed, but it wasn't an unhappy sigh. There was something so delicious about the ordinary. When I got back to the farmhouse, I would write to Charlie and tell him all the ordinary things I'd been up to that summer … and maybe one day I'd tell him about the extraordinary things as well.

As the gates opened and we left Otterly Park, Dad patted my knee. "I'm glad you took us, Katie. It's amazing what you can learn in an old house like that."

I smiled out the window as if Sophia could see me and share in the joke.

"It sure is." And as I said it, my fingers wrapped around the golden locket hanging around my neck, a treasured secret resting close to my heart.

ACKNOWLEDGEMENTS

A book is a magical thing: a story is born to the world that never before existed, a portal to a new world that readers can visit time and time again! I could never have created the magic of this book on my own. It seems terribly unfair that only my name appears on the cover when, in reality, *so* many people deserve a bit of the credit. And so, I shall do my best to dish out some of that credit to its rightful owners:

Enormous thanks to my Beta Readers who have shared in this adventure from my earliest spark of an idea: To my greatest fans and coincidentally my parents, Jim and Mary Blume; Marion and Tamysn Alston; Alex Thaxton; and my partner-in-story-crime Bri Stox. Yours were the first eyes to read this book, and your encouragements gave me the courage to run with it.

Special thanks to you, Bri, for rooting me on through the NaNoWriMo challenge that resulted in *Katie Watson and the Painter's Plot.* I would never have dared it without you!And special thanks to Alex, my expert consultant for all things horse related. Vagabond is indebted to you, and Miss Thaxton the riding instructor deserves an adventure story all of her own.

More special thanks are due to Katherine Parham, my oldest friend and Katie's namesake. So much of Katie and Sophia's friendship is inspired by our childhood adventures. And to Yesim Yemenici, your enthusiasm and thoughtful comments helped me see this book as a true work of art.

Next, a round of applause for my insightful editor Anna Bowles for helping this novel reach its full potential, for Patrick Knowles whose stunning cover design is truly a work of magic, and for my proofreader Michelle Bullock who helped get the book squeaky clean and ready to greet the world.

To all eight of my brilliant, fear-defying nieces, you inspire me, and Katie Watson is a hodgepodge of you all. A special nod to you, Amelia, because your hankering for an adventure one summer was, I think, what first brought Katie to life.

This fledgling book would have little chance of taking flight without my amazing Launch Team: (besides those already mentioned) Jo Wallis, Hannah and Caitlin O'Keeffe, Fiona and Izzy Kennedy, Phillip and Eileen Blume and Jasmine, Rachael, Amelia and Anna Grant, Rebecca, Abby, Sophia and Nora Davis, Natasha, Jasmine and Maia Fenner, Ruth Nelson, Megan Pressley, Michael Dormandy and many others!

Several wonderful, *real-life* places make appearances in this book disguised under different names: Thanks to the National Trust's Knole House (Otterly Manor) in Kent, and

Horse Guards Parade at St James's Palace (the stables at Otterly Manor), for providing inspiration!

Last but certainly not least, I'd have thrown in the towel on this whole writing thing long ago without the constant bucking-up I get from one Gordon Stead. Thank you, dear, for the visits to Knole House that first sparked off this story, for being a shoulder in the dips along the road to publication, and for celebrating all the little victories with me. Thank you for believing this day would come even when I was sure it never would. You win!

GET THE AUDIOBOOK FREE!

Enjoyed reading *Katie Watson and the Painter's Plot*? Now you can have it read *to you* by the author!

Visit the link or scan the QR code to download and listen to the audiobook for FREE!

http://eepurl.com/dcp6Bj

ABOUT THE AUTHOR

Mez Blume grew up in the United States, spending every moment she could in the forest. At age 21, she followed her nose to England and got an MA in Gothic Cathedrals at the Courtauld Institute of Art. Mez lives in West Berkshire with her husband Gordon and Jack Russel Terrier Hugo. She still spends every spare moment in the forest.

For more information visit:
www.mezblume.com

Made in the USA
Columbia, SC
28 July 2020